Wisdom on the Green

Smarter Six Sigma Business Solutions

Forrest W. Breyfogle III
David Enck
Phil Flories
Tom Pearson

www.smartersolutions.com
Austin, Texas

Resounding Praise for
Wisdom on the Green

"An easy read, but powerful in its ability to give the reader the essential points of effective Six Sigma techniques, beyond the math and equations of other books. Its use of golf and work analogies makes the points seem real and tangible." - Bob Ashenbrenner, former Director of Engineering, Dell

"The best business book I've read all year. As a former IBM Principal and business consultant for Global 1000 and mid-sized businesses, I am urging all of my clients to grab a copy of *Wisdom on the Green.* Forrest [and team] have done a masterful job of using a golfing metaphor to translate the concepts of Six Sigma business methods--as practiced by such noted authorities as Jack Welch of GE-- into language that any manager or executive can quickly grasp and apply. Given my current handicap, I will not only be taking this book to the office but also to the golf course!" - Frank Shines, Former Principal, IBM global Services

"An easy-reading but insightful overview of how to use proven techniques to improve bottom-line performance." - Fred Bothwell

Wisdom on the Green

Smarter Six Sigma Business Solutions

Wisdom on the Green
Smarter Six Sigma Business Solutions

Printed in the United States

10 9 8 7 6 5 4 3 2

Publisher's Cataloging-in-Publication
(Provided by Quality Books, Inc.)

Wisdom on the Green : Smarter Six Sigma Business Solutions
/ Forrest W. Breyfogle III ... [et al.]. -- 1st ed.
p. cm.
Includes bibliographical references and index.

ISBN 0-9713222-0-1

1. Business--Fiction. 2. Quality control--
Statistical methods. 3. Production management--
Statistical methods. 4. Golf--fiction. I. Breyfogle,
Forrest W., 1946-

PS3600.AW57 2001   813'.6
                                QBI01-700907

Author Dedications

To Bill Diamond who introduced me to DOE and Stan Wheeler who mentored my use of statistical methodologies. – FB

To my wife, Kathy, for her love and support – PF

To Sandy who taught me that logic and science are only half the answer. –TP

To my wife Gayla, whose love and support have helped me pursue my dreams, and my parents who raised me to have dreams to pursue. –DE

Contents

Preface

This book follows four successful friends who met in graduate school while pursuing their MBAs. Now they meet for a monthly golf outing to continue their friendship, discuss their careers, and compete in a friendly golf game for the price of dinner. The challenges they face in business and in their personal lives are all too familiar. Golf provides an intriguing metaphor for the game of life, with its complexities and challenges, changing conditions, chances for creativity, penalties, and rewards. Moreover, golf is the game most often associated with business. As Hank, Jorge, Wayne, and Zack share their experiences and pursuit of improvement in *Wisdom on the Green*, they discover powerful new insights that help them see how they can improve their games, both in business and in golf.

This book will focus on the implementation of Six Sigma as a business strategy. Part of this strategy will include the integration of the Lean Enterprise philosophy with that of Six Sigma. We will also discuss ISO-9000:2000, Malcolm Baldrige Assessments, Total Quality Management (TQM), Balanced Scorecard, and Theory of Constraints (TOC).

For implementation of Six Sigma, we will describe our strategy, which we call *Smarter Six Sigma Solutions*[SM], or *S⁴* [SM]. This step-by-step roadmap has evolved over the years within the training and coaching sessions conducted by *Smarter Solutions*[SM], Inc. An initial roadmap for this methodology is described in *Implementing Six Sigma*[1] and *Managing Six Sigma*[2].

The *Smarter Six Sigma Solutions* strategy calls the highest-level measurement a *Satellite-Level*[SM] Metric, which is for tracking the high-level business measures to which Six Sigma projects are aligned. This approach also uses *30,000-Foot-Level*[SM] Metrics to track Key Process Output variables (KPOVs) of projects. These metrics are useful for establishing a baseline for Six Sigma projects, detecting when project change has occurred, and giving a high-level control measure that can monitor overall process change during and after a project is completed. To make improvements, focus is given within Six Sigma projects to identifying one or more Key Process Input Variables (KPIVs) that affect the KPOV variable. With the S^4 approach, many KPIVs are referred to as *50-Foot-Level*[SM] Metrics, which are used to control the KPOV(s).

The mathematical relationship $Y=f(x)$ is sometimes used within Six Sigma training to represent the principle that in a system, outputs are a function of inputs. In Six Sigma terms: KPOV=f(KPIV).

Some how-tos will be included within this book; however, we will reference other books, articles, and websites that give more in-depth descriptions of implementation.

The glossary elaborates on both technical and golfing terms used within the book that may not be familiar to all readers.

***

Comments and suggestions for improvement to this book are greatly appreciated. Please send your input to forrest@smartersolutions.com.

Smarter Solutions, *Smarter Six Sigma Solutions*, S^4, *Satellite-Level*, *30,000-Foot-Level*, and *50-Foot-Level* are service marks of Smarter Solutions, Inc.

Wisdom on the Green

Smarter Six Sigma Business Solutions

Chapter 1: The Starting Point

The Waggle

The waggle is ... a small practice swing and a way to ease tension.

Bobby Jones said if you saw him waggle more than twice, he probably hit a bad shot.

Harvey Penick's Little Red Book

March

Hank arrived early at the golf course and was hitting some balls to loosen up. The sky was crystal blue, and the wind was still. The weather was perfect for 18 holes of golf, but Hank was having a hard time getting his mind off work.

As Vice-President of Operations at Hi-Tech Computers, his background in electrical engineering and an MBA had helped make him a fast tracker. Hi-Tech was an aggressive, successful computer component manufacturer with plants in the Southwest US and Mexico. Recently, however, it had been facing new competition and pressures from its biggest customers to comply with growing regulations, improve delivery times, become more flexible, and lower prices. Of course, they all wanted perfect products as well. Things were really heating up. Hank again tried to concentrate on golf.

Hank was tall and strong at 46 years old. He looked more like the former linebacker he had been in college than a PGA pro. He loved golf, but all attempts to improve on his 12 handicap seemed to fall victim to a few big numbers each round. If he could just eliminate those big mistakes, especially the penalty strokes for out-of-bounds and unplayable lies, he was sure he could achieve his goal of consistently breaking 80. After all, he thought, he could hit the ball a long way and often made great shots. He had a hole-in-one and a flock of eagles on his resume, but he could also hit it into trouble on the very next shot. If he could just eliminate the double bogies (and worse), he would be happy with his game. Hank forced a resigned smile as he promised himself to practice more and to try harder this year. If work would ease up just a little, he could blitz this game. Hank loved to "grip it and rip it", the exact opposite of his regular playing partner Jorge, who thought his way around the golf course as well as in the boardroom at Harris Hospital.

Hank thought for a moment about the possible root cause of his big numbers. Sometimes he hooked the ball, sometimes he sliced it, but usually he hit it pretty well. Once in a while it was dead-solid-perfect. He was proud of his ability to scramble, to recover from trouble, both on the course and when fighting fires at work. He just wished for fewer of those big mistakes that cost him extra time and constant reorganizations at work and penalty strokes on the golf course. Yes, the increasing pressure from Hi-Tech's customers, shareholders, and regulators was eating into his golf practice time. Recently, more "snowmen", those nasty

8's, were showing up on his scorecard than he cared to admit.

He was still engrossed in his thoughts when he saw his old college buddies, Jorge, Wayne, and Zack, walking toward the practice green. Their tee time was still 20 minutes away, so they caught up on family news as they practiced. Zack, always the serious one, was even able to slide in some business discussions about the latest investment model his company was developing that would produce a high rate of return with minimized risk. Meanwhile, he rolled in another long practice putt. Jorge was hitting a few of his magic chip shots from the fringe, while Wayne stretched and warmed up his smooth, rhythmic swing with his 7 iron.

***

As they approached the first tee, they agreed to their usual pairings: Hank and Jorge teamed against Wayne and Zack in a game of two-man best ball. The best individual score on each team determined who won the hole. The team that won the most holes could win the front nine, the back nine, and total. Loss of two out of the three meant you picked up the tab for dinner. Hank liked this game. He could play his own ball and keep his own score, make an occasional great shot, and still rely on steady old Jorge to carry him on a hole if he came up with one of those big numbers. The game had provided lots of camaraderie and good-natured competition over the years.

After winning the coin toss for honors, Hank stepped to the first tee and surveyed the 425-yard par 4. He didn't like this hole. It's not that he didn't like a challenge, but he preferred a simpler par 4 that gave him a chance to warm up a bit on the first hole. This one was long and hard, demanding immediate execution from the very first swing. Closer inspection showed a Mexico-sized bunker guarding the next 75 yards along the inside of the dogleg about 150 yards out on the right side of the fairway. About 100 yards off the tee, a stream that today looked like the Rio Grande crossed the fairway. "Get those negative thoughts out of your head," Hank thought as he made his first swing. The muffled "click" told him immediately that he was in trouble. His new ball cleared the Rio Grande but disappeared weakly into the heart of Mexico.

Jorge was up next and hit a modest drive that ended up short but in play. Wayne stroked a beautiful 275-yard drive that successfully avoided the hazards that had befallen Hank, and then Zack hooked a drive into the light rough on the left.

Zack chided Jorge and Hank, "Looks like you guys will be picking up the tab tonight."

As they rode to their second shots, Jorge said, "Hank, you better get rid of that slice. I know it's been a while since our last game, but I don't want to lose to these guys again."

Hank bit his lip. He didn't have a slice problem. He just wasn't warmed up yet. He changed the subject. "My mind is still at work and not on this lousy game."

Hank stepped out of the cart and selected a 3 wood. It was a very difficult shot, but he was still 300 yards from the green, and on a long par 4 like this, Jorge would never be able to reach the green in two. Hank didn't want to start off too far behind in this match. His mind was churning, and his swing was rushed as the mighty blow took mostly sand. The ball trickled only a few yards ahead, still in the trap. Hank's blood pressure rose as he hit the next two shots only a few yards each. Now he had really done it. Blown the first hole on his way to another 8 or worse. There were still 40 yards of sand in front of him. Hank took a deep breath and tried to ignore the barbs flying from the other golf cart as he stepped out of the trap and exchanged his 3 wood for his trusty 5 iron. It wouldn't make it to the green, but it should get out of the trap and get him back in play. A mediocre swing advanced his ball out of the trap, just barely to the point where he had expected to find his original drive. "Four strokes wasted... I've done it again!" Hank fumed to himself.

As he climbed back into the cart, Jorge calmly said, "Why didn't you just chip the first one sideways back out into the fairway and save yourself a few strokes and a lot of grief?"

Hank fought back the urge to snap at his partner just long enough to realize the wisdom of his advice. He did that too often... threw good strokes after bad, compounding his original mistake by blindly charging straight ahead. How could someone who hit the ball no better than Jorge play him almost even? On most holes, Hank thought, he easily outplayed Jorge, but on a few holes each round Jorge would take a scrambling par or routine bogey while Hank exploded to a double bogey... or worse. When the final scores were tabulated, Jorge was almost always closer than you would expect and sometimes even beat Hank. Was there a smarter way to play this game? Was Jorge on to something?

As Hank tried to reason it out, he forgot about the comments coming from Wayne and Zack and began to settle down. When they reached his ball, he hit a smooth 6 iron on the green and two-putted for another dreaded 8. Fortunately, Jorge had scraped the ball along, getting close in three, hit another great chip shot within inches, and made the tap-in for bogey. Meanwhile Wayne and Zack seemed distracted, and made bogey as well.

"Hank, you better get your head in the game, or we're gonna end up paying for dinner," Jorge prodded him.

"I told you that my mind is still at work," Hank responded.

"So what's the problem?" Jorge asked.

"I've been pressuring my managers to increase profit margins. They did it, all right, by shifting most of the connector assembly work to a couple of our plants in Mexico. The problem is that another manager discovered that our division had a component supplier inside Mexico with an even lower cost structure and decided to move half of the production to that plant."

Wayne who had been listening in on the conversation at the second tee empathized with Hank. "We are running into the same problems at Wonder-Chem. As with every company, there is always constant pressure from the Wall Street analysts to reduce costs and increase quarterly profits. Meanwhile, it seems like there's always another problem surfacing. For example, last month we had a major yield hit which held up delivery of our shampoo products to our northeast distributors due to a container defect. Our engineers were trying to cut costs with a new injection-molded container; however, the side wall of one of the corners was too thin, and 300,000 shampoo bottles leaked all over our warehouse floor when a cold front moved through."

Hank continued his story. "After transferring the equipment and operations, they found out that the third plant lacks the necessary quality and safety certifications, and it's not even set up to ship product to the United States! It's been a colossal screw-up!"

"Why didn't these issues surface when your management was researching lower-cost alternatives?" Jorge asked as he lined up to hit his driver on the second tee.

Watching Jorge, Hank remembered how long it always took his friend to prepare for his shot. "We could be out here all day," he thought, and decided to hold his reply until his partner finished. After all, there was a hefty dinner bill riding on the match.

Jorge waggled gently side to side, readjusting his stance, trying to avoid the inevitable. The driver had always been his weakest club, and it pained him each time he reached for it. As expected, Jorge didn't break any driving records, but the ball went 175 yards straight down the fairway.

"You really need to get over your driver phobia if we're ever going to finish this round."

"Well, at least **I'm** on the fairway," Jorge responded with a slight smile.

"Whatever," Hank replied. "As I was saying, the management in Mexico assumed we knew about the certification and delivery issues. They were in the process of laying out a plan to ship product to a US plant using a certified freight forwarder that could ship between the US and Mexico. Can you imagine? They actually planned to use a middleman to ship product from Mexico to a plant in Oklahoma and then turn around and ship from Oklahoma to our customers!"

As he told the story, Hank began to burn with anger, "Our management team has spent the last two days developing a plan to meet current orders from our existing plants and move production back to the original two plants in Mexico. Instead of saving cost and labor, we've added millions to our expenses this year."

***

Once his story had been told, Hank began to refocus on his golf game. With his obligatory "snowman" out of the way, he actually played pretty well, recovering to shoot 85. Jorge struggled on the long holes but teamed well when Hank faltered to finish with 89. Wayne was solid as ever with his 76; just a few missed putts from shooting par. Zack used his wonderful putting stroke to stave off total disaster and finished with 96. Hank and Jorge lost the front side by one hole, but recovered to win the back nine holes by two and win the overall match. Later that evening, as Wayne and Zack split the dinner tab, Hank relived Jorge's beautiful 20-foot putt on the 18th green, which sealed their victory.

He was even able to tell a version of the old golf joke on himself. "Hey, Hank, how did you make 8 on the first hole? I just missed a 30-footer for my 7!"

Hank's friends wished him luck in solving his production problems. They all knew that Hank was really at his best when fighting fires. The interesting part would be hearing about his solution.

On the drive home, Hank thought about his good friends. There were many interesting similarities among them. They had played together for years, ever since they met in MBA classes at the university. They were all

24

competitive, in golf and in business, and Hank thought it was no coincidence that they had all advanced to VP level in their respective companies. However, each had some unique traits.

Jorge was 47 and a Senior Vice President at Harris Hospital. Short and stocky, with a choppy golf swing due to an old soccer injury to his shoulder, he was good at keeping the ball down in the wind. He used his typical fade to great advantage as long as the shot did not require too much distance. His real trademark was his short game. Too often, it seemed Jorge was chipping on and one-putting while Hank was on in two and three-putting or worse. It wasn't so much that Jorge was a great putter; he wasn't as good as Zack, but he just didn't leave himself very many long or hard putts.

Wayne was 45, and a VP of Research and Development at Wonder-Chem. He had leveraged his BS in Chemistry and MBA to manage product development successfully for the last few years. Wayne had the look of the former basketball player he had been, even though he was not especially tall. Fortunately, he had been a great shooter and a starting varsity guard in college. His conservative haircut, clothes, and bifocal glasses made him look more like an accountant than a scientist, but his precision golf swing was a thing of beauty. Ten years earlier, Hank had joked that he was going to invest for retirement by sponsoring Wayne on the Senior Tour when he reached fifty. Back then, Wayne had been almost a scratch golfer, but age seemed to be taking its toll. For several seasons Wayne had not putted as well, and his average had slipped into the upper 70s. That was good for the group competition; at least they didn't have to play 3 against 1 as they had in the beginning, but Hank wondered what had happened to Wayne's game.

For that matter, what had happened to his own game? He had slipped a few strokes as well, and now Jorge was beating him more often. He thought again about Jorge's "lesson" on the first hole today. It would bear more investigation.

Finally, there was Zack. Youngest of the group at 44, he looked even younger. He had the muscular build of a baseball player and the baseball swing to go with it. He was the most erratic of the group until he reached the green. Then the magic started. His eagle eye could read putts with the best of them and he spent lots of time practicing on the putting green. No one drained as many putts as Zack. Fortunately for Hank and Jorge, he was usually already out of the hole by then.

Yes, it was a good group. Good friends, good competition, good people. Unfortunately, as Hank pulled in the driveway, he remembered his problems at work and began to worry about what he would do next.

Chapter 2: The Mexico Meeting

Do You Need Help?

If you play poorly one day, forget it.

If you play poorly the next time out, review your fundamentals of grip, stance, aim, and ball position. Most mistakes are made before the club is swung.

If you play poorly for a third time in a row, go see your professional.

Harvey Penick's Little Red Book

One Week Later

Things were happening fast for Hank. One week after the golf outing he found himself on the way to Juarez, Mexico for a weeklong business trip. There would be many hours of meetings once he arrived, so he allowed himself a moment to relax and to think about the golf outing. Surprisingly, he had shot a pretty good score. It would have been very good if it hadn't been for that 8 on the first hole. Maybe there was a lesson in Jorge's comments. Still, hindsight is usually 20/20. Once you have wasted three or four shots in a bunker, it's easy to say you should have played a safe shot out of the trap rather than risk a heroic shot with a 3 wood. Still, he could have made that shot. He'd done it before. Not that often, but he **had**! How do you know when to take a chance and when to play it smart? The odds of making the more difficult shot are lower, but the possible rewards are much higher. Did Jorge know the odds? Were the odds different for players with different skills? Should you always try to do what the pros would do, or should you sometimes take Jorge's advice and play it smart? Jorge was good at thinking his way around the course. He certainly did get more out of his limited physical skills than Hank. Did he just play more or was there really a solution that was smarter? Hank decided he should study this further, on the golf course, naturally.

Suddenly thoughts of the Mexico meeting played through in his mind. Not only did he need to find a solution to the current production problems; he also had to address the original business issues that led to the plant transfer in the first place. The plants needed to reduce costs and increase throughput to stay competitive in their market.

***

On Monday morning, Hank met with his new manufacturing director, Karen Johnson, and the production supervisors from the Mexicali and Juarez plants, Juan Rodriguez and Carlos Silva. Hank wanted to discuss how to salvage the current situation. Karen was a manufacturing engineer who had become a good manager. He liked Karen and trusted her judgement.

Just hours prior to the meeting, Hank had learned from an email that production at the Juarez plant had not been impacted by the move. Operations at their second plant in Mexicali had been transferred to a plant in Mexico City.

He also discovered that the original plant in Mexicali was not completely shutdown. During a five-hour marathon meeting, they decided that the best solution would be to transfer operations back to the Mexicali plant from Mexico City.

The complete waste of this undertaking was painful. Equipment transfer costs, lost sales, and setup costs were just the tip of the iceberg in terms of damage to the bottom-line. In preparation for its closing, they had also lost some of their best employees through layoffs at the Mexicali plant.

***

By Thursday morning the operations meeting was complete, and the business unit review was set to begin. The other key managers for the business unit flew in Wednesday night.

Because of a re-organization, the members were all new; however, the least-experienced member had been with the company for ten years so at least they weren't novices. The new members included John Jenkins, the supply chain manager; Ellen Simpson, the quality manager; and Andy Anderson, the marketing manager.

Hank opened the meeting with a clear plan in mind. "The purpose of this meeting is to define the problems of this business unit and develop a plan to solve them. I want to know all of the important problems you're facing. Anything not brought up today cannot be used as a crutch for future poor performance. Let's start with marketing."

Anderson stood and walked to the front of the room like a fifth grader who hadn't completed his homework. "Well," he stammered, trying to collect himself while pulling out a collection of slides and placing the first one on the overhead projector, "as you can see from this slide, we have gone from a 50 to 35% market share over the past year." To his surprise, Hank said nothing. Anderson was expecting some browbeating over the poor performance, even though the deficiencies were due to his predecessors.

Anderson collected his thoughts and continued, "This reduction in market share is due mainly to three new competitors who have entered the market. This competition has turned the sub-assemblies we make into a commodity item. Customers are no longer willing to pay a premium for our brand name."

Hank responded in an even tone, "I would challenge some of your conclusions; however, the purpose of this meeting is to discover problems. Is there anything else?"

Anderson was thinking fast. He hadn't expected to get past the 15% drop in market share, not with Hank's temper. Everyone was scared of Hank so they didn't always give him the complete story, but his reaction hadn't been so bad. Maybe he could tell him about the product delivery problem.

Here goes nothing, Anderson thought, as he pulled out his next few slides and continued his presentation. "We're also losing customers because our delivery times are not meeting their needs."

"Wait a minute," a shout came across the table. Rodriguez was on his feet in a flash. "That's not true! We have a near-perfect record of on-time delivery."

Anderson responded, "That's because our sales representatives tell customers our lead time is three weeks. Customers who need their product sooner don't order or they are forced to wait three weeks and then don't re-order with us. Our competitors have a shorter lead time and..."

Rodriguez interrupted again, "But why didn't you say something!" Rodriguez was beside himself due to what he considered an unwarranted attack.

"We did!" Anderson responded forcefully. "If you had been listening..."

Hank interrupted them, "Okay, I see the problem. We'll work it out later. For now we're just defining the problems. Let's hear from supply chain next. John?"

Jenkins relaxed a bit as he stood. Maybe there would be no executions today after all. He spoke from his position at the conference table. "We have supplier and delivery problems. Our suppliers sometimes run out of inventory when we have a big order, and at other times we have weeks of inventory. Due to the complicated bidding process for our suppliers, the purchasing group head count has increased. Our delivery contractor can't seem to provide consistent delivery times and tends to lose orders on a fairly regular basis. Unfortunately, we are forced to use that particular contractor because purchasing negotiated a contract for the entire business unit."

"Is that it?" asked Hank. Jenkins nodded. Hank then asked Juan to summarize the key Juarez production issues.

Juan stood and started through his list of problems. It seemed as if Hank had heard them all before: large finished-goods inventory, large amount of work in process, not enough storage space, changing schedules, missing parts, and quality problems.

Finally he finished, and Hank asked, "Is that all?" and Juan nodded.

"Great, now how are we going to fix these problems, people?" Hank asked with a steady, even stare.

No one said a word. Hank decided to wait for an answer.

After three minutes of silence that seemed like an hour, Carlos spoke, "When working for my previous employer, we used a different production method. It was called Lean Manufacturing, and it seemed to address many of the problems we discussed today."

Hank had heard of Lean Manufacturing and had even read some on the topic. After further discussions, Hank decided that he would look further into Lean Manufacturing techniques, but for now he was exhausted, and, he knew, so was everyone else in the meeting.

***

Hank was glad to be home. The trip to Mexico had been grueling, but worthwhile. Now all he had to do was learn how to implement a Lean Manufacturing system, he thought with a smile. He decided to give himself Sunday off. After all, those problems would still be there Monday. Today, he would keep his other promise to himself and work on his golf. Driving to the practice range, he thought back over his last few rounds and tried to remember his worst holes. He was sure that if he could improve on those two or three really bad holes each round, even if he just turned them into bogies, he could save 2 or 3 strokes on each bad hole. That could easily make an improvement of five or six shots per round and get his average down close

32

to 80. That would mean some rounds in the seventies. Look out, Wayne!

But how could he avoid those big meltdowns? If he followed Jorge's advice and always took the safe shot, he would give up any chance for the occasional great shot that got him a birdie or eagle. That seemed counter-productive, and not nearly as much fun. He paid for a large bucket of balls, and decided that his driver set the stage for success or failure on most holes. A good long drive usually meant a chance at par or birdie, and it felt great when the others in the group "ooh'd" and "aah'd" over one of his really big hits. He smiled as he thought about last summer and the drive he had smoked 325 yards, followed by a beautiful 125-yard 8 iron, which fell for an eagle! They still talked about that one. On the other hand, he often hit a bad one like he did on the first hole at the last outing, got in trouble, and quickly degenerated to a double bogey or worse. Maybe he should just practice more with his driver. As he set the balls down on the range, he reached for the "big dog" and started to work. It was his favorite club. He'd work it out.

***

After a few phone calls on Monday, Hank was able to contact Lean and Mean Manufacturing Consultants (LMMC) and in short order was speaking with the president, Jason Sanders. Hank wanted to know more about Lean, and Jason was happy to give him a summary.

Jason started by talking about lean production. "Lean production is a philosophy of how to conduct production. Even though the techniques originated in manufacturing, the ideas can be used for service or transactional processes.

33

Even new product development can benefit from the methodology."

Jason continued, "Lean manufacturing is a set of techniques used to implement the Lean production philosophy. The Toyota Production System or TPS, as it is sometimes called, is a good example of Lean production. Toyota has been developing its production philosophy and implementation tools since the 1950s."

Hank took the following notes on some basic principles of Lean Production and Lean Manufacturing tools:

- Don't overproduce: Make what the customer wants when he wants it. This holds true both for internal and external customers
- Define customer value: Root out non-value-added activity
- Focus on the entire value stream (supply chain): It does no good to reduce the time it takes to produce a product if the delivery system accounts for 80% of the product delivery time
- Convert from batch processing to continuous flow whenever possible
- Synchronize production between process steps
- Develop ability to make your full product mix in any given day
- Relentlessly pursue perfection

Tools used to implement the Lean production philosophy include:

- The 5S procedures used to clean-up and organize a work place (house keeping)
  1. Sort
  2. Straighten
  3. Shine
  4. Standardize Work
  5. Sustain Improvements
- Store inventory close to where it will be used in production.
- Reduce Setup Time
  This impacts the ability to make every part every day
- Implement Production Cells
  Production cells are picces of equipment that are organized so that product can flow from one piece of equipment to the next during production. They work well when implemented with small batch sizes and pull production. This methodology also works well for non-manufacturing activities, such as development and transactional projects.
- Utilize Kanban Production Control
  Kanban production characterized by a small collection of inventory parts between each production workstation and no work done by a process step until the next process downstream uses some of the stored inventory.

What the Lean Manufacturing consultant said made sense to Hank. He would delegate the details of implementation to someone else in the organization while he oversaw the progress. He made a note to contact his Manufacturing Director, Karen Johnson, to have her meet with Jason to start putting an implementation plan together immediately. Hank smiled to himself as he hung up the phone. He liked working with Karen. She was smart and efficient. They would attack this problem head-on and solve it together.

He relaxed for a moment and thought about golf again. Maybe Lean could help there, too. Could it help eliminate those wasted second, third, or fourth shots? Hitting that bucket of balls on Sunday had certainly not helped much. Sure, there were some beautiful shots that turned heads on the range, but deep down Hank knew that at least ten percent of his drives were still unacceptable. That would have cost him strokes (rework?) on the course. Then he thought about Jorge's advice again and could not erase the feeling that there was something important in it.

Chapter 3: Methods

Putting

One thing all great putters have in common, regardless of their style, is that the putting stroke is approximately the same length back and through.

With short putts concentrate on the line.

With long putts concentrate on the distance.

Harvey Penick's Little Red Book

April

Hank could hardly contain himself as he worked his way down the winding road from his house to the golf course. He was eager to tell his friends about the new program that he had implemented to solve the manufacturing problems in Mexico.

As he traveled the familiar route to the golf course, he randomly thought about his business. How many reorganizations had he done in the last three years? Was it four or five? Well, no matter, if the current leaders couldn't cut costs and increase throughput, he would just find someone who could.

To Hank, business was a form of combat. The object was to create a winning strategy, deploy your forces, and execute to plan, thereby destroying the opposition. In many ways it was just like football, Hank thought. After the fiasco last month, he had had to shake up his organization again. As he arrived at the golf course, his thoughts turned to the details of his current method of combat, the Lean Manufacturing Program.

Meanwhile, down on the practice green, Wayne watched the crowd gather to observe the spectacle that Zack and Jorge had created. They were betting on who could make the longest putt. They had started with five-foot putts and worked their way up to 15 feet. Jorge was completely focused, ignoring everyone at the moment. He knew every break on this practice green, and a lot was riding on this putt. He had just bet Zack leadership of the free world that he would sink this 25-footer.

Just as the putter started forward, Hank came down the hill yelling greetings to his friends. Jorge's concentration was remarkable as he stroked the putt and watched the ball gather speed down a slight incline, and then break three feet left to right just as he had predicted. Reaching the hole, the ball caught the far side of the cup, executed a complete 360-degree wrap around, and hung on the edge. A noticeable sigh rose from the assembled crowd. Then, just as everyone had given up on the shot, the blades of grass underneath the ball gave way, and the ball dropped into the cup.

Everyone around the green was cheering. Jorge was surprised at how much he enjoyed the accolades. As he smiled to himself, he thought, "Was it the putt or the fact that I've regained control over the free world?" Actually, it was the putt; neither he nor Zack had ever bothered to place an operational definition on what they meant by control of the free world. Jorge wasn't sure what he had won. In the end he just enjoyed the competition.

"Great putt," Hank called out, "but save a few of those for our match, partner. Hey, you guys won't believe what's happened at work since last month!"

Jorge stopped him in mid-thought, "We're not going to start talking about work right away, are we? How 'bout talking about my beautiful putt for now?" he said with a laugh. Hank agreed impatiently to hold shoptalk until later.

***

By the fifth hole, Hank's earlier excitement began to resurface. While waiting for Zack to find his ball in the thick rough down the left side of the fairway, Hank again started to explain what had happened in the last month. "After the fiasco, I re-organized the manufacturing group and brought in a new director. Then I had her initiate a Lean Manufacturing program."

"From what I've learned about Lean Manufacturing, we should be able to respond more quickly to product-demand changes, reduce costs, and increase our throughput," Hank continued.

"I found my ball," Zack yelled. "Do you believe this rough? I almost needed a hedge trimmer just to get to my ball," he joked. At this point, the group wasn't paying any attention to Zack as talk had turned strictly business.

Hank continued, "All kinds of problems have brought our business to the brink of extinction. In order to develop a game plan for saving the business, we held a management review and decided to start a Lean Manufacturing program."

Wayne was getting interested. He had recently started discussions with his management team about what program they could initiate to help solve some of their company problems. Low yields, poor on-time delivery, raw material issues, and high costs were just a few of the chronic problems Wonder-Chem was facing. Wayne asked, "How will Lean Manufacturing reduce costs?"

Hank spent the better part of the 9th and 10th holes explaining what he had learned from Jason, his Lean Manufacturing Consultant.

Wayne explained that they had decided to bring back the Total Quality Management (TQM) initiative that Wonder-Chem had tried some years ago. Their slogan had been:

Wonder-Chem is committed to being a company of the highest quality in every aspect of its business activity.

There had been some good, isolated results from the TQM program, but not enough to capture upper management's attention or sustain the program.

In retrospect, Wayne felt the major problem with TQM was that the Quality Department had been chosen to implement it. Wonder-Chem's quality organization could be very hard-line and uncompromising with respect to how they viewed problems. They seemed to have no concern for overall business issues, with their total focus placed on Quality. As a result, the Quality Department had a hard time getting operations managers to cooperate and let their people join the Quality Improvement Teams. Wayne remembered one meeting in particular during which the TQM program leaders demanded more top-management support and financial resources to address a long-range improvement, while ignoring the hard business reality that the funding they were requesting would severely impact production operations.

"This time I am going to do it differently," Wayne explained. "I am going to hire a program leader who can cooperate with all of the departments within the business. This person will also have experience in product development and manufacturing. I'll make sure that the team leaders within the TQM group have experience in other parts of the organization."

"TQM really was a good initiative," Hank interjected. "In fact, we went through TQM training some years ago and got some good results here and there."

Zack walked up complaining about his horrible shot. "This hole is going to ruin my round. This isn't my typical game."

"Not your typical game?" chided Wayne. "Every time we play, you run into several holes that kick your butt. Maybe you need a new driver, one you can keep in play," he said with a sly grin.

For an instant, Hank was distracted from the business discussion. Zack had lots of flaws that cost him strokes; what he needed was a new swing. He thought for a moment about his own game. Maybe one of the new over-sized titanium drivers would be just the cure for his bad hole or two each round.

Then Zack switched topics to offer his perspective on the business discussions. "One of our directors started measuring his division against the Malcolm Baldrige

41

Award criteria, and has been very excited about the prospects, so I decided to expand the program company-wide."

"I've heard about the Baldrige criteria but don't really understand what they entail," Hank responded.

"The criteria comprise seven categories. Let's see, one was leadership. Another was planning. A third was business results. I think there was one on customers. I can never remember them all, but they cover everything, and a perfect score is 1000. You evaluate each category and add up your total score," Zack answered.

"Measurable criteria sound good, but haven't some companies that won the award gone out of business or had financial problems?" Wayne interjected.

Zack responded anxiously, "Are you sure about that, Wayne? Joe didn't mention that when he was describing all the benefits."

"I'm pretty sure that's the case," Wayne replied.

***

As the others continued to talk about their programs and the promise they saw for improvements, Jorge said nothing. He thought that his company didn't need programs. Jorge believed that his people worked hard. He also thought his rapport with his entire management team allowed him to handle problems on a personal level. And he certainly had some problems to work on.

Reduced HMO payment schedules had forced Jorge to develop a cost reduction program within his hospital. After hearing about Hank's problems with his plants in Mexico last month, he had carefully pointed out to his managers that they needed to protect the patients' interests during any cost reduction initiative. He was confident that the cost reductions wouldn't pose any problems. He had a great pool of talent on his management team, and they were all very committed to their patients.

As they approached the green, Jorge was farthest from the cup. He strode across the green, feeling the springy *give* under his feet that you get on well-maintained golf greens. It was like those rubberized surfaces used for running tracks. He wondered who came up with that idea of combining crushed tires with asphalt to create those spongy track surfaces. He was always fascinated by such creativity and was continually looking for someone with that spark to add to his team.

"Okay," he thought to himself, "back to golf." As he read the break of the green, Zack called out another leader of the free world challenge. If Jorge sank the putt, he could maintain his rule. If not, Zack had an opportunity to become Supreme Commander on his next putt. Once leadership changed hands, the other could regain power only through another challenge. Jorge was always up for a challenge, especially around the green.

After sinking the 25-footer, Jorge gave Zack a good-natured ribbing for even thinking he could challenge the master. Zack conceded that Jorge was master of the green, for now anyway.

While waiting for the others to putt out, Jorge wondered why Zack never challenged Hank or Wayne. Maybe it was because Jorge and Zack were acknowledged as the best putters in the group. Hank and Wayne were long-ball hitters. They were always giving each other a hard time about a short or missed drive.

It occurred to him that they all seemed to focus their practice on their strengths. Hank and Wayne almost never showed up early on the putting green. They were always at the driving range. Likewise, he never went to the driving range. After thinking about it, he decided that the best way for him to take strokes off his score would be to practice the part of his game that offered the most opportunity for improvement. For him, it wasn't just how far he could hit the ball; it was positioning the ball on the fairway. He had a very good short game, but most of his skill was used to overcome poor ball position after his tee shot.

***

Later, Wayne ruined a routine par hole opportunity with an agonizing four-putt and complained, "I think I'll go buy one of those new One-Shot putters that I saw at the clubhouse. I haven't four-putted in years."

Jorge just smiled, remembering some years back when they were playing regularly. Wayne had bought three new putters in one year to help "fix" his putting. He was still at it.

Just then, everyone jumped when Jorge's cell phone rang. After a brief but animated conversation, Jorge returned to the group. "What's going on, Jorge? I've never seen your face so red," Wayne asked with real concern.

Jorge had a hard time collecting his thoughts. After a moment, he was able to explain his panic in a coherent manner. "There has been a major problem at the hospital. A change in saline bag labeling and sizing caused a whole floor of patients at the hospital to be over-medicated."

He went on, "Doctors are on their way, and I have to head over to help organize our patient protection plan and notification of appropriate government agencies. So far, everyone is okay, thank goodness. However, there are notifications and paper work that have to be handled very carefully to avoid any further allegations of incompetence and cover-up."

Jorge jumped into his cart and headed for the clubhouse as his friends wished him well. They headed for the next tee a lot more somber than they had been just moments ago. Their match was suspended, and they would finish the round without much enthusiasm.

Driving back to the clubhouse, Jorge began collecting his thoughts. He was greatly relieved to hear that none of the over-medications was life threatening. Still this was a very serious problem. How could something like this happen? Who dropped the ball? Jorge thought long and hard on these questions. Was it his fault for pushing for cost reductions? Was it the administrators' fault for notifying only the supervising nurse of the first shift? Was it the nurse's fault for leaving town in the middle of the night to be with her husband who had suffered a heart attack? Was it the inexperienced nurse who selected the wrong size bag due to a change in labels?

Jorge made it to his car on autopilot, but he was still trying to sort out just what had happened. It seemed like such an unlikely string of events. Why, how, he couldn't seem to decide. He was in a painful loop of self-doubt and managerial rage. He decided to put it out of his mind until he got more information at the hospital. After all, there would be plenty of time to try to recover from this mess in the coming weeks.

While driving, Jorge tried to focus on the oldies' radio station rather than his current problems. Too bad the music he grew up with was now known as oldies. He started thinking about all the musicians he used to listen to as a young man. It was amazing how many musicians started out and how few found their big break. And for the bands that made it, there was always some interesting story about their hardships along the way.

Didn't all musicians think that they were talented and hard-working? And believed that they would make it? But most didn't. It seemed like it was almost luck of the draw. With so many bands starting, one had to get a break.

Then it hit him like a 300-yard drive right between the eyes. The over-medication was not a fluke event. Having some problem is inevitable; it's just a matter of which problem occurs. There are literally thousands of potentially deadly events that can occur every day in a hospital. All operations, medications, and critical information transfers are like potential musicians trying to get their big break. Some problem will occur sooner or later by chance.

For any critical activity there are numerous chains of events that can cause some horrible outcome. Given so many possibilities, even good people doing their jobs well can have problems unless processes are designed to be error-proof. Of course, whenever those problems are reviewed later, the chain of events looks so specific and unusual that everyone believes they were unique occurrences.

Often, we do not recognize that it is the system which allows the failures to occur. The better the system, the less likely a failure will occur. Jorge chastised himself for not realizing this before. In fact, he had presided over task forces that had solved many specific problems. When the task force was done, the members patted themselves on the back for fixing the problem. They then handled the next problem as though it were an independent issue, missing the system connection between them.

Furthermore, the way the process was set up, all of the obvious high-risk areas had backups. He wondered how many times the backup systems saved a life with no recognition that the backup procedure was even used. After all, if the backup saved someone's life, technically that's still a failure, costing time and money, of the original system. Then, with enough failures of the initial process, even the backup systems were likely to fail at some point. There were also other potential issues that might not seem as deadly on the surface, but if you combined a number of failures for these secondary issues, the result might be deadly.

His revelation helped ease his anxiety somewhat; however, having this understanding was still not enough. How could this have been avoided? He kicked himself for not having implemented some type of improvement plan like that of his friends. He hadn't thought he needed it. His problems were different; they were information-related.

Now he knew he did need something, but what? The programs his friends were talking about seemed a lot like Wayne's new putter or Zack's new driver. They reminded him of his discussions with his managers: isolated efforts to solve disconnected problems. What he wanted was to change the process of how people did their jobs. That was the only way to head off all the potential failures in the system.

As Jorge pulled into his parking space, he realized he was shaking. This was **his** hospital. These patients were in his charge, and he was responsible for their well being. He had almost had a catastrophe, the magnitude of which he didn't want to contemplate.

All right, he told himself, steadying his hands as they rested on the steering wheel; it ends here. We will change how we do business. Patients will not have to fear for their health when they enter our hospital. And we will still reduce our costs so that we can provide affordable care. Just how this was going to happen he wasn't sure yet, but it would.

As he climbed out of the car, some doubt started creeping back.

Chapter 4: Initial Issues

The Short Game

The higher your score, the faster you can lower it – with the short game.

For two weeks devote 90 percent of your practice time to chipping and putting...

and your 95 will turn into 90. I guarantee it.

Harvey Penick's Little Red Book

May

It was mid-morning on a beautiful Saturday, and Wayne was sitting outside the Pro Shop at a picnic table, enjoying the cool morning breeze and a cup of coffee. He had arrived at the golf course early to hit some balls at the driving range, and his swing was in fine tune. Now he was just waiting for his friends to arrive. That was the good news. The bad news was that every golfer in the state, it seemed, was either on the course already or in line in front of them. Wayne tried to prepare himself mentally for a long day of slow play. Concentration would be a challenge today. If they had not all been so busy at work, they could have played during the week.

In fact, it had been a long week, a long month for that matter. His management team was working hard to get the TQM program established. They had hired a new TQM director, updated and revised the training materials, and developed a new training plan.

He had high hopes for TQM and was disappointed at the response the program generated during its initial six weeks. Earlier in the week, he had visited some of the training sessions unannounced and found only half of the scheduled managers present.

Engineers and other employees who were required to attend were unhappy about middle management not buying into the program. They expressed concern openly, worried that their managers wouldn't know how to utilize TQM techniques nor understand the time burden it placed on their employees.

Wayne agreed with his employees' concerns and the next day instituted a sign-in sheet for management. He couldn't believe he had to resort to this, but attendance did pick up as a result. However, he wondered if this was really a long-term solution, or if managers were just going through the motions by attending the sessions. He certainly hoped his managers were committing to the program; the company really needed to cut costs and improve the performance of their over-the-counter health care products. In the long run, they also needed to reduce development times for their prescription drugs.

Wayne contemplated his company's loss of market share over the past couple of years. Marketing had not been able to reverse the decline, giving excuses that prices were too high.

Jorge and Hank showed up five minutes before their scheduled tee time, interrupting Wayne's thoughts of future cost reduction and improvement ideas. No one had heard from Zack, and rather than giving up their tee time, they proceeded without him, hoping he could join them later.

***

An hour later, Zack caught up with his friends who were waiting to hit on the fourth tee and engaged in an agitated conversation. Wayne was gesticulating wildly, as Zack arrived just in time to hear the trailing part of his sentence "… and the managers weren't even showing up to the training."

"Hey Zack," Jorge called out, grateful to change the subject, "where've you been?"

"I went to the office to take care of some documentation," Zack replied. "We've been implementing the Malcolm Baldrige assessment program throughout the company so we can determine where to focus improvement efforts. It's taken a lot more work than I expected. All last week I was in Baldrige-training with my analysts, and I spent all morning sorting out some scoring consensus issues."

Wayne stopped mid-stride as he was finally stepping onto the tee, turned towards Zack, and proclaimed, "What a great idea! If I went to classes and some of the team meetings, my managers would know I'm serious about our TQM program."

Wayne launched a slight draw long and down the middle of the fairway, and Zack continued, "This Baldrige

51

assessment program is going to be great. By observing where we stand relative to the standard, we will know where we need to improve. In fact, this could help take care of the type of problem that you had last month, Jorge."

Jorge wasn't listening; instead he thought about how this particular hole was easy to play, with a wide fairway that would accommodate the variety of slices and hooks that their foursome usually produced. As luck would have it, he hit the ball straight and long, with just a hint of power-fade. "What do you mean, Zack?" Jorge asked with a smile, obviously pleased with his shot.

"The Baldrige evaluation would have pointed out that the change control process for patient medication was not error proof. The only difference between your processes and ours is that ours deal with customers in the financial services industry instead of with medication and patients," Zack explained while lining up to swing.

After Hank and Zack had also hit good shots, they all congratulated each other and started down the fairway. Jorge thought about the unusually good outcome and how many times the four had teed off together over the years. Sooner or later, they were all bound to hit the ball long and straight on the same hole … and this was that rare moment.

Zack continued as they headed down the fairway, "In each of our three divisions we have a Baldrige-trained champion and some experienced people to lead the charge. All the directors are responsible for making sure the managers set up teams to perform Baldrige evaluations. There's been a lot of complaining, but we keep telling people we need to understand where to improve so that customers are satisfied and we meet our strategic goals."

"Have you noticed any improvements yet?" Jorge asked as he walked towards his ball.

"We have approximately 900 people in 25 different departments within my company. Each department will be evaluated. So far, we've only completed five departments in the six weeks; but two weeks were taken up in training. I haven't noticed any improvements yet, but we're still in the evaluation phase," Zack elaborated.

Jorge listened intently as he selected a 9 iron to travel the 100 remaining yards to the green. His compact swing was ideal for short-iron play and produced a near-perfect shot with ample backspin that covered the pin placement cut on the front of the green. Jorge's ball landed ten yards beyond and slightly left of the hole, bit on the soft green, hopped backward five feet, and rolled back right towards the pin. Hank yelled, and Wayne ran to get a better look. The ball stopped four inches short of the cup. Zack congratulated Jorge while Hank and Wayne both exclaimed that it should have gone in.

Jorge was pleased. An eagle on a par 4 would have been a career shot, but he hadn't hit the target. Still, he had come close, and that's what he had wanted to do. He would happily settle for an easy birdie.

***

After his great approach shot, Jorge was able to carry some momentum through the next two holes, where he recorded a par and another birdie on a par 3. He wondered why he was doing so much better the last few holes. He was wondering if it was luck or real game improvement, when a bogey and a double bogey on the next two holes provided his answer.

With the excitement of golf greatness over, Jorge's thoughts wandered from the game back to work. He wondered why his friends hadn't asked him about the problem that forced him to leave early last time. Perhaps they were each consumed with their own work problems.

Jorge then asked, "So Hank, you haven't spoken much about the Lean Manufacturing program you started. How's it going?"

Hank replied, "Actually it's called Lean Enterprise. Lean Manufacturing is only one part of the whole program. Lean Enterprise looks at the whole value stream. So if your supplier is the reason your deliveries are late, you fix the supplier rather than try to speed up the manufacturing cycle time."

Hank continued, "But to answer your question, it's not going as well as I had hoped. Lean has all of these great tools and approaches. We should be able to use them to reduce costs and lead-time, but I'm not seeing results. I even hired a director of Lean Manufacturing and appointed a steering committee. We recently held a site-wide meeting at the manufacturing plants where this is being implemented."

"You're up, Hank," Wayne said, prodding the group to keep moving. It was easy to get sidetracked when play was slow, he thought.

Hank pulled his driver from his bag, as he explained to his friends some of the problems he was having with Lean. "I went to some training classes and had an experience similar to Wayne's: half the managers weren't in class; they were off fixing problems. When I asked why, they said training was nice when you have time, but they had real work to do." In addition to the buy-in issues, Hank explained, there were problems with spotty implementation. Even where some implementation had taken place, he couldn't see any tangible results.

Wayne grew impatient as he waited for Hank to swing, but Hank continued to discuss the issues he was experiencing with Lean Enterprise. He spoke of the results of various teams. One team conducted some 5S activities, with no visible results. Another team conducted some Kaizen events. Although this had produced some localized results, Hank could not confirm how the claimed results would impact his business metrics. Optimistically, he told his friends that it would just take some time, and that some of the advanced techniques would have greater impact.

***

The 16th hole was a wicked 527-yard par 5 with a double dogleg and a creek that crossed the fairway twice. Trees on both sides of the tight fairway gave weekend golfers plenty of chances to shed old golf balls. While the group waited to tee off, Zack finally noticed that Jorge was about to tee off with a 3 iron.

When asked why, Jorge answered with a sly grin, "I haven't hit a driver all day long!"

"But what about that great drive on number 4 that set you up for the birdie?" asked Hank.

"That was my 3 wood", Jorge smiled. "I'm tired of fighting my game. I don't want to have to make difficult second shots continually to save a hole after a bad tee shot gets me in trouble. I used some organizational wisdom to list out the reasons for my bad holes and decided that it was my erratic driver."

Wayne laughed, "Organizational Wisdom? What's that?"

"It's a term I learned from the Six Sigma training I've been going through at work," Jorge replied. "Organizational wisdom comes intuitively from what you know about a process due to past experience. At work we use organizational wisdom to come up with ideas on how to improve our business processes. I just evaluated my golf game using my own organizational wisdom based on past experience."

Jorge continued, "My biggest problem seems to be my tee shots. Bad tee shots are killing me. It doesn't matter how good my short game is; too often, my drives are bad enough that I can't recover. I decided to leave my driver in the bag today, and I have had only one double bogie."

Zack questioned, "But Jorge, you hit some good drives, too."

Jorge elaborated, "I looked at the distribution of my drives in both distance and accuracy. Over the last ten years I have played over 300 rounds of golf. When I really thought about it, fewer than 20% of my drives are really good enough to get me in position to make par or birdie. About two-thirds of them leave me in some degree of trouble, and on about half of them, I can salvage a par or bogie with my good short game. The other half the time I have to struggle just to save bogie. The rest of my tee shots are so bad that even my short game can't save me and I'm facing double bogie or worse. By making smarter decisions on my tee shots, I may be a little shorter off the tee, but I'm more predictable. I can plan my attack better, and reduce the chances of falling apart on a hole. I guess you could say that I've made my process more robust."

Zack said, "What do you mean? Have you been working out?"

Jorge laughed and said, "No, I guess you could say I am just working 'smarter'. The term 'robust' refers to the concept of picking a process, in this case the club I hit, that has a normal variation pattern well within the allowable limits for the task. You are familiar with error-proofing, of course. Well, when we can't error-proof the process completely, the next best thing is to be robust. In golf, that means picking the club that has the highest probability of landing in an acceptable spot with respect to both direction and distance. If my 3 iron has a 90% chance of keeping me in play for par, and my driver only has a 30% chance of doing that, my process for making good drives is more robust with the 3 iron. Even if the driver gives me a slightly better chance for birdie by going farther, it has a much higher chance of going into a hazard or out-of-bounds. 'Course management' is at least partially 'risk management'. It depends on the situation."

With that, Jorge hit his 3 iron off the tee, 175 yards down the middle, just short of the creek, in good position for his second shot.

Zack looked incredulous, "Where did you come up with all this?"

"Our Six Sigma training inspired this change " said Jorge.

Wayne interrupted, "Six Sigma? What's that?"

"Six Sigma was started by Motorola and made popular by GE. Recently, some companies have dramatically impacted their bottom-line through the completion of projects that are aligned to the strategic goals of their business. The people who drive these projects are called Six Sigma Black Belts," Jorge answered.

"Six Sigma Black Belts? Is this some kind of martial art?" Wayne interrupted again. He grinned as he noticed that Hank seemed to like that idea.

Jorge continued, "No, Six Sigma Black Belts are trained to work with teams and tackle problems systematically. After the over-medication problem we had last month, I knew we had to do something different. I had read some articles about the benefits of Six Sigma and decided to do some investigation."

Jorge calmly stood over his second shot in the fairway, and split the fairway a second time with another beautiful 3 iron, that went 170 yards, stopping well short of the second creek crossing, right in the opening of the dogleg for his approach to the green.

"How did you pick between service providers?" Wayne asked.

"I made some phone calls and did a lot of searching on the internet. I found a couple books that had a step-by-step process for implementing Six Sigma. At first I thought we could use these books to implement Six Sigma on our own. After further investigation, I realized we needed some expert advise to get started. I interviewed several Six Sigma providers and then chose ours because they had a unique approach that helped us align our projects with our business goals. In addition, they had a practical roadmap for executing successful Six Sigma projects. Most importantly they were not jumping on the recent Six Sigma bandwagon, having been established for almost a decade," Jorge elaborated.

When they reached Jorge's ball, he hit a **third** perfect 3 iron to within a few yards of the front of the green. After some delay looking for Zack's ball in the left rough, they finally made their way to the green.

When it was Jorge's turn, he smoothly chipped his 7 iron into the front of the green and rolled it to within eight inches of the cup. Hank, who had hit a monster 285-yard drive, had hooked his approach shot into the trees and scrambled for a bogey. Wayne hit two beautiful shots and a half wedge onto the green before three-putting again for a bogey. Zack's ball went unfound in the trees, and with the penalty strokes took an 8.

As they waited on the 17th tee, Jorge finished his story. "When I decided to go with Six Sigma I learned that I needed organizational buy-in at all levels to get it to work. I appointed a steering committee and brought in our Six Sigma provider to organize the implementation. We conducted executive and champion training sessions."

Zack interrupted, "What are champions?"

Jorge continued, "Champions are executive managers who remove barriers that Black Belts encounter when executing their projects. We are now training twenty Black Belts, which consists of four one-week training sessions that are conducted over four months. Each trainee has a project that is worth at least $100,000 to the business."

"Defining and scoping-out projects are essential. Management decided what major functions were most critical, what specific processes within the functions were important, and how to track the Key Process Output Variables or KPOVs of the process."

"Like everyone else, we're having some buy-in problems. However, I know that our current projects are aligned with our business strategies and will show results. The results are what will get everyone on board."

As the group waited on the 18th tee, Hank thought for a minute, and then said, "Maybe I should leave my driver in the bag, and avoid my double bogies too."

Jorge smiled and said, "All of our games are different. Before you decide on your game improvement methods, you really need to measure and analyze your own game. I'm sure you'll find that, on many holes, your driver is a formidable weapon. You just need to understand the percentages."

Hank then said, "At least, I think I'll check out your Six Sigma methods. Can you get me started?"

"Sure," Jorge responded.

On the 18th green, Jorge snaked in a ten-foot side-hill putt for 79! It was his best score in several years, and his driver had never left the bag. He even beat Wayne, who shot 80.

As Jorge bought a round in the clubhouse, they all agreed that it had been a very long day, almost a six-hour round, but somehow, everyone felt like it just may have been worth it.

Chapter 5: Continuing Problems

The Challenge

Like chess, golf is a game that is forever challenging but can never be conquered.

Harvey Penick's Little Red Book

August

It was late on a hot, muggy Friday night in August, on the eve of the monthly golf game. Zack sat sulking in his office. Why couldn't he figure out why customer complaints were still going **up?** True to his nature, when things started going bad, Zack had taken personal responsibility for fixing the problem. However, it seemed as if every time he and his team fixed one problem, several new ones would appear to take its place. It was as if he were trapped watching continuous reruns of the old movie *Gremlins*. Every time they killed off a defect, several unpleasant little relatives seemed to appear. The thought of skipping the monthly golf outing with his old college buddies crossed his mind, but he hated it. Because of vacations and weddings, the foursome hadn't met since May, and he was way past ready for a little break.

Z-Credit Financial had recently developed a system to capture customer complaints and respond within 24 hours with an action plan for closure. Then, when complaints continued to come in, Zack dove into the details of the tracking system. He was trying to assess whether people had really been conducting root-cause analysis and following up on action items. It seemed like the proper procedures were being followed, and yet wrong addresses and incorrect balance transfers were still frequently occurring defects.

Zack wondered why his implementation of the Baldrige assessment program hadn't led to fewer customer complaints. There was always something else going wrong, and overall things were not improving. At one in the morning, he found his coffeepot empty and decided to give the investigation up for the night. He tried to think how he could start fresh on this in the morning and knew for sure that he would be missing another round with his friends.

On the drive home, Zack's mind wandered toward the golf game he would be missing tomorrow. Jorge's magical round was the last real success story he could remember. Maybe Wayne was wrong. Maybe he didn't need a new driver. Maybe he should change the way he approached the game, and leave the driver in the bag like Jorge. But what about all the other shots that got him in trouble? Whenever he worked on one part of his game, defects popped up in other areas to kill his round. What had Jorge said to Hank at the end of his round? Something about each of them having different games and the need to analyze your own game before deciding on an improvement strategy.

As Zack entered the driveway of his home, he noted that the lights were out. Liz and the kids had finally given up and gone to bed. The cold supper in the fridge and the dark house didn't seem like the payback he was hoping for. Maybe if he got started early tomorrow, he could still salvage some time with his family on Sunday.

***

During the last two months, Hank had also been experiencing problems with his Lean Enterprise program. One implementation team was able to reduce batch size on one of the manufacturing lines, but defects caused confusion and problems to the point that there was actually more Work-in-Process (WIP) inventory than when they had started. Some of the process cycle times had improved, but the overall cycle time to get a part through the system has increased considerably. Several of his key customers were now reminding him that the real business metrics were established and measured by the customer.

On another process, a Kaizen event was conducted in order to reduce manufacturing cost for a particular product by addressing the setup time for a sheet metal punching operation. The team was able to reduce setup time from an average of two hours to 15 minutes by setting up the punches outside the press. Even though there were hidden problems with increased labor costs, the team truly believed that they were successful because set-up time was reduced. Hank knew that the overall business improvement was negligible so far, but he hoped that even a perceived success might motivate his team.

Hank felt like he was back calling the defensive plays in college again. Whenever he moved people up to stop the run, the opponent would pass. When he dropped back into coverage, the opposition ran over them. When Hank decided to blitz from his linebacker slot, they would dump a screen pass over his head. He needed a better system then, and he needed one now. He hadn't been able to talk to Jorge since their last round, but now he was eager to know more about Jorge's systems approach to improvement, both for business and for golf.

***

Meanwhile, Wayne had growing concerns about his TQM program as well. Two projects were finished, but the problems that they had solved were not high on the priority list of strategic goals for the business. A lot more projects were coming up, but he was not sure of their business value either. Overall customer satisfaction had not improved, and teams were not spending enough time on their projects. Wayne had been burning a lot of midnight oil trying, in vain, to determine why TQM had not given him the results he expected. The teams were well-organized, and seemed to be motivated, but they just couldn't seem to see the key relationships between the processes that they could control and the business outcomes they needed.

Wayne removed his glasses and rubbed his eyes. On these long days, he could hardly read the detail reports, let alone see any key process relationships. He was getting a headache. Maybe he needed new glasses. Karen had been pestering him about having his eyes checked. He'd make that appointment as soon as he got over the hump at work. Too bad he didn't know anyone who could give his TQM program a vision check. His mind drifted towards his family for a minute. Karen was a great mom to Mike and

64

Shelly. It had to be tough now that they were both teenagers. He needed to spend more time with all of them. He really needed to get this TQM program running on its own. Wonder-Chem needed more results, and his family needed more of him.

***

Unlike his friends, Jorge was making significant progress with his Six Sigma business strategy. Several of the teams had found some unexpected low-hanging-fruit opportunities for improvement. Even better, these projects were well aligned with the strategic goals of the business, making the project benefits even more visible. This seemed to excite and motivate other teams to work even harder on their projects as well. Some real momentum was building.

Personally, Jorge was elated with the results. He learned that some of the statistical analyses his teams were doing had indicated there were many common cause issues intrinsic to their processes. Previously, these issues would probably have been interpreted as special causes, events unusual to the process. Fire-fighting would have ensued, and often the almost random fixes would have masked real root causes and may have made overall system performance worse. Now, his teams were able to pinpoint those areas where overall system improvement was required, and have a better idea how to proceed. Jorge's organization recently created metrics for Harris Hospital that separated common cause from special cause. Now his teams were learning how to make long-lasting improvements through fixing the process, not just fire-fighting the problem of the day.

Jorge leaned back as he visualized how a Six Sigma perspective could apply to many additional areas of his business. He could see the way that improvements-through-projects were affecting how his people viewed their processes in terms of the overall business results. The thought of expanding it throughout the business was exciting. Jorge, always the system thinker, thought this was a great business improvement system.

Jorge stretched and relaxed for a moment, thinking about dinner tonight and golf tomorrow. He deserved a break, and tonight's dinner with Sandra should be a great start to a good weekend. He was taking Sandra to their favorite place, a quiet little restaurant they had found when they first met. Thinking about Sandra made him smile. She was a beautiful lady and a very successful career woman. He'd learned so much from her. When he was studying pre-med, he had learned to reason in the logical/analytical style of a scientist. Later, his MBA classes taught him to think in terms of business systems. But when he met Sandra, he was amazed to find her to be very successful even though she seemed to rely almost entirely on her powerful intuition and understanding of human nature. Over the years, their discussions had taught him that his logic did not always lead to the right answer, and that Sandra was right at least as often as he was. Now he relied on her wonderful intuitive senses to augment his logic and systems thinking. Together, they made quite a team.

His mind wandered a bit further, thinking about creativity and wondering if that was what *thinking out of the box* was really about: suspending traditional logic and analyses long enough to consider possibilities that did not seem to compute logically. He thought about the many times as a scientist and businessman that he had seen long-accepted theories disproved in favor of new illogical theories. Yes, he decided, good business management is a combination of science and logic, business and finance, and people's creativity and intuition. The trick was to treat it as a system.

Chapter 6: The Discussion

The Three Most Important Clubs

The three most important clubs in the bag, in order, are the putter, the driver, and the wedge...

A good putter is a match for anyone. A bad putter is a match for no one.

Harvey Penick's Little Red Book

August

Hank and Jorge stood alone near the first tee early Saturday morning. "Too bad about Zack and Wayne," Jorge lamented. "At least these two fellows they paired us with look like they can hit the ball."

"You would think Zack and Wayne could get out for a round of golf," Hank replied sarcastically. He didn't know if he was mad at them for not showing up or for working while he was playing. He worried about the time away from the office and wondered if he should be working as well.

As they waited to tee off, Hank started thinking about Six Sigma. He was impressed with Jorge's success with the program and was wondering if it might complement his Lean Enterprise program.

Hank remembered what Jorge had told him at the last outing, specifically that Six Sigma was not a program, but a statistically-based business improvement methodology, which eliminates large problems and improves operations. Jorge was emphatic about Six Sigma's equating to how people *should* do their jobs, especially at the executive level. Since the last outing, Hank had been doing his homework and had a lot of questions for Jorge. "I've done some reading, and everybody says that Six Sigma is just for engineers to reduce defects on manufacturing processes. Is the major goal of Six Sigma to achieve 3.4 defects per million operations or something called DPMO?" Hank asked.

Jorge responded, "That's what you often hear from people who don't really understand the process. The DPMO metric was created by engineers, but there are a lot of statistical measures and methods that apply to both manufacturing and transactional situations. The statistical tools and methods help us to prioritize what's important, better understand our current important processes, evaluate potential solutions, and make sure that the improvement holds.

"What role do managers play in the success of Six Sigma?" Hank wondered aloud.

"Management's task is to create the infrastructure, remove barriers, and make improvements happen," Jorge continued. "When you asked the computer components group to cut costs, you expected the individual managers to reduce their expenditures, reduce head count, cut discretionary spending, and reduce inventory. Standard stuff, right? With this type of thinking you were set up to fail sooner or later. People worked independently within their own responsibilities trying to solve the problem. Nobody was looking at the bigger picture, which resulted in havoc for your Mexico operations."

Hank listened intently as he took his driver from the bag. He settled in to his pre-shot routine, and took a smooth but powerful swing. The results drew positive exclamations from Jorge and the two new partners, as a long drive with just a hint of draw pierced the fairway. Hank worried silently for an instant that he might have hit it too well, and gone through the slight dogleg into the first cut of rough.

"If you had a team that approached this as a systems issue, a more effective solution could have been found. The problem may have been prevented instead of corrected after it occurred. A broader picture could have offered a bigger and more permanent solution. Six Sigma Black Belts are trained to start with a very broad view and work their way towards the details," Jorge continued as they approached Hank's drive.

"I don't believe it!" Hank yelled from a couple feet away.

"No, it's true," replied Jorge, astonished at his friend's harsh reaction.

"Oh no, no," laughed Hank. "I was talking about my lie; I'm almost buried in this rough. How can the first cut be this thick?" He pulled a 5 iron from his bag as he said, "If I can get out of this rough in one stroke, it will be a miracle. Actually, I'm interested in hearing the rest if you don't mind me stealing your ideas."

"Why did you pick that club?" Jorge asked, seemingly more interested in Hank's club selection.

Hank responded, "I'm about 170 from the pin. My 5 iron normally goes a bit farther than that, but I expect to have trouble getting out of this buried lie."

"Yes, don't you normally hit your 5 iron more like 185 or 190?" Jorge questioned. Without waiting for an answer he continued, "Remember my decision to leave the driver in the bag last time? I did that to minimize the variation in my tee shots, so I could predict where I would land more accurately. Through better club selection I can make my shot process more robust to the normal variability in my swing. With this approach, I could depend on good ball positioning to make pars or save bogies. If you hit that 5 iron cleanly, you'll go over the green into the trees. If you don't, you won't reach it anyway, and you'll land in one of the front sand traps."

"OK," Hank said with a flash of interest, "what do you suggest?"

Jorge offered, "If you hit a 9 iron, you will almost certainly get out of the rough and land in the open area just in front of the green. Then pitch on close and make your putt for par. You're looking at a tap-in for bogey 5, worst case. But if you leave that 5 iron in the rough, or pull it into the trees, you're on your way to another 8. What do you think?"

"Or maybe I should have hit my 3 iron off the tee, stayed short of the dogleg, and hit my 5 iron to the green in the first place?" Hank added.

"That would have been good, too, but now that you're here, make the best of it. Plan ahead and keep the overall goal in mind. It's not always about maximizing the current shot at any cost. Remember, they don't ask **how** at the end of the day, just **how many**?" said Jorge.

After Hank hit a solid 9 iron to within 20 yards of the front of the green, Jorge continued, "I was thinking about the problems you had in Mexico. A Six Sigma solution wouldn't even have started with your statement that you wanted to reduce costs by moving operations. First, you create a list of the company's most important objectives, and they provide the definitions for Six Sigma projects. Executives communicate organizational goals and appoint Six Sigma teams to define projects that are aligned with these goals. Suppose the cost reduction was the most important problem and you assigned a team to attack the issue. They wouldn't start to reduce costs by studying the individual budgets of the groups involved. Rather, they would ask a number of questions. How do we define and measure cost? What is the nature of variability within our cost structure? What categories make up the entire cost structure for production in this division? What categories offer the greatest opportunity for overall cost reduction? For a given category, what components add to that category's total cost?"

Hank was a little puzzled. He interrupted, "This sounds like a great system, but what about DPMO? What's the Sigma level? Why haven't I heard this before?"

"This strategy started out in technical areas, and 3.4 DPMO was the appropriate metric for the problems those folks were solving. When it started to gain popularity, that single metric was easy for people to convey."

Hank thought carefully about what Jorge had just said, "I've been thinking about all the times I told my people to solve some huge problem and didn't give them this kind of a process to make the job doable. Think of all the opportunities for huge returns if we get some of these teams on the chronic problems we've been fire-fighting for ever."

Hank was good with his wedge. It was a strong point in his game. He hit a pretty pitch shot that landed on the front of the green and rolled to within four feet of the flag. With his confidence up, he drilled his par putt and then asked Jorge the big question, "So I should start teeing off regularly with my 3 iron?"

Jorge laughed, "Of course not. Your big drives are a great weapon in your arsenal. But golf is a target game... distance **and** direction. Think about the target area that you need to hit with each shot. What are the limits of acceptable errors in distance and direction? Then pick the best club to hit. Not by the longest distance you have ever hit it, but the range of distances you normally hit it. And don't forget the range of direction errors you normally make. For your driver, I'd bet most of your shots travel 220 to 280 yards."

With this, he handed Hank a picture he had just drawn on the back of the scorecard. It was the familiar normal distribution with a mean at 250 yards and standard deviation partitions marked off in 15-yard increments. Jorge then said, "Plus and minus two sigma only cover about 95% of your drives. 205 to 295 would cover 99.74%. Your 370-yarder last year was a pleasant 'outlier'. These are just estimates, of course. You can refine them with measurement and analysis. But if you had thought about the likelihood associated with various driving distances, you might not have selected a driver back there where the far side of the dogleg was only 260 yards away."

"Of course," Hank's insight flashed. "I should think of my golf swing as a process where key process outputs that I want to control are distance and accuracy. A key process input variable to this process is choice of clubs. For my swing, each club produces a distribution of shots with a range of distance and directional accuracy. I should pick the club most likely to give the best response for each operation... I mean shot."

"Now you've got it," smiled Jorge. "There will be times when you have plenty of open space and your driver will be a terrific weapon. Just pick your spots wisely."

***

Later, Jorge said, "In Six Sigma there are a couple of underlying principles that all employees can use within their job to improve their efficiency. First they need to understand the big picture. They next need to know what the customer wants, both internal and external customers. They also need to reduce variation and drive to target."

"Didn't you say something about this is the way people should do their jobs? Until now, we've been discussing teams that go after specific problems. Where does the continuous improvement come in?" asked Hank.

"These ideas can be used to improve your company's processes on an ongoing basis without causing chaos like you experienced in Mexico. It's pretty clear that the manager didn't understand the big picture or the voice of the customer when he made the decision to change plants on the basis of component cost alone."

Hank agreed as he looked at the picture on the back of the scorecard again at the next tee. Then he looked at the hole and saw a small landing area for the drive that was only about 30 yards in diameter, about 200 yards from the tee. He reached for his 4 iron as Jorge smiled.

"Take my business," Jorge continued. "Our Customer Service Representatives (CSRs) are supposed to keep track of patients' billing records. Historically, we had CSRs separated by functional area: Each would work in emergency, hospital or physical therapy. It seemed like a natural way to do it because each CSR would become familiar and efficient with the area-specific procedures. After taking two weeks of Six Sigma training, one of our less-experienced CSRs suggested we combine CSRs into one functional area. This would allow all CSRs to see how each area addresses issues, allow us to back each other up, and actually reduce head count by five employees."

"That's amazing!" Hank commented. "Why would someone make a suggestion that could put him out of work?"

"Because we personally assured everyone at the beginning that any improvements would not result in the loss of jobs. We explained we would retrain displaced workers to enhance their skills. Job reductions would only occur through normal attrition. The worker that made the suggestion was re-trained for an area we knew was going to need people in the near future."

"This sounds great, Jorge, but you haven't really told me how this works. I would need to hear more of the details about the infrastructure and how the project teams function. And what about Lean Enterprise? Was that a waste of my time? How about TQM, Baldrige, and ISO-9000, for that matter? How do they fit in? What do you know about Theory of Constraints or TOC? Does that fit in with your Six Sigma process, too?"

"Tell you what, Hank. I'll explain the connection of Six Sigma with the other programs while I take you on for the rest of the round. During lunch, I'll lay out some of the basics of the Six Sigma infrastructure and project execution. Remember, I've only been at this for about three months now, so I don't know all the details, but I can give you the big picture."

"Sounds great," Hank said. "Now what about the connection to Lean?"

"Actually, Hank, I've heard different answers to this question. It depends on whom you ask. Most companies that start with Lean believe that you do Lean first and that leads to the application of Six Sigma tools to reduce defects. Six Sigma proponents often say it works the other way round. They tend to believe that after Six Sigma is implemented, you can address work-flow issues using Lean methodologies."

"Our Six Sigma consultants had a different spin on things. First, they proposed a high-level business metric and project metric. They call the business metric the *Satellite-Level* Metric and the primary project metric the *30,000-Foot-Level* Metric. Using the *Satellite-Level* Metric strategy, business track measures like return on investment and inventory levels on a monthly basis. As part of this strategy, the *30,000-Foot-Level* Metrics could track project or operational metrics on a daily basis and are designed to get you out of the fire-fighting mode."

Hank responded, "Sounds great!"

Jorge continued, "When common cause variability is unsatisfactory, you need to systematically improve the overall process, rather than chasing daily problems. The tools you select to fix the process depend on your situation. If the problem were from waste or muda, you would probably use Lean tools. Other situations require Six Sigma tools, and some even require both."

"What about Kaizen?" Hank asked.

"People often include these techniques in their Lean implementation. Our instructor described one company, which said that they did a Kaizen Event every other week and saved $10,000 per event. This might initially sound impressive, but do you think it's real?"

Hank paused for a moment, "If the boss told me to save $10,000 per event, I bet I could make it look like I did."

Jorge responded, "Exactly. However, what happened during the Kaizen event might be detrimental to the entire system. For example, one cell could have improved its efficiency and piled excess inventory in front of the next cell of the process, creating a bottleneck. At the end of the day, the overall system was degraded for localized gain."

"The *30,000-Foot-Level* Metric view of a process can lead to Kaizen events when appropriate. This approach keeps you from spending a lot of time and money on Kaizen events that don't benefit the overall business."

"Where does TOC fit in?" Hank persisted. His questions were endless.

"TOC can also be a big help within a Six Sigma business strategy. It can identify and model constraint areas that need improvement through Six Sigma projects."

Hank responded, "Sounds like we could use Six Sigma to meet our ISO-9000:2000 requirements as well. With the 2000 version of ISO-9000, we now not only have to document our processes but we have to show that we're improving them."

"The question is what do you do? Do you need to improve all your processes or just the critical ones?" Jorge asked.

"I certainly wouldn't want to try to improve everything. Some areas just aren't as important as others and don't need improvement," Hank replied.

"The great thing about this is you could reference your Six Sigma Business Strategy as the methodology for improving your organization per the ISO-9000:2000 requirement. With this approach, you can leverage your improvement activities to the needs of the business," Jorge added.

"What about the people who say Six Sigma is just TQM repackaged?" Hank wondered.

"TQM is different. Typically, TQM was set up as a separate entity within an organization to solve quality problems. Six Sigma is meant to be used by upper management to direct strategic change," Jorge explained.

"I have this twenty-foot putt for a birdie to win today's round. I believe you'll be buying lunch, or would you rather put the leadership of the free world on this?" Hank commented as he stroked the downhill putt through two breaks and into the cup.

Hank turned with a satisfied grin and headed to the clubhouse. As he walked off, he heard Jorge call after him, "That's another premise of Six Sigma: if you putt enough times, you're bound to make one sooner or later. Even a blind squirrel finds an acorn once in a while."

Chapter 7: It's in the Details

The Average Golfer

Sometimes I wonder, what is an average golfer.

I read somewhere that... the average male golfer shoots about 92.

I don't believe it. Not if he counts every stroke and plays by USGA rules.

Harvey Penick's Little Red Book

That Same Day Over Lunch

Hank thought about the comment Jorge made about his putting. After the initial irritation, he thought he saw the point. We remember our once-in-a-lifetime shots. Sometimes they just happen, but that doesn't mean we should plan on hitting a career shot every time.

Jorge's discussion about the Six Sigma strategy started the wheels turning in his head. He wondered why he not heard of this before? He had always discounted Six Sigma as just another quality-improvement program, mostly because of the 3.4 DPMO discussions, but now he was thinking otherwise.

Hank was frustrated that he had not tried earlier to understand Six Sigma better. The opportunities seemed endless. The idea of people improving the way they do their jobs excited him. As he waited at the table for Jorge, he was anxious to learn more. Jorge certainly seemed to be doing well with it so far. He'd find out more details over lunch.

***

Jorge found Hank at a table by a window with a beautiful view of the golf course.

"What took you so long? Did you three-putt?" Hank teased him from across the room. "Tell me the details about how Six Sigma works. I remember you told us about the training and the need to set up an infrastructure. What did that entail?"

Jorge responded, "We started by establishing a steering committee which selected the Champions and Black Belts. As we continue to roll out our Six Sigma business strategy, we are learning that we will need to add Green Belts, which are part-time Black Belts, to help implement projects."

Hank nodded and asked, "What about project execution? How is this any different from the Plan-Do-Check-Act approach? You know, the one that Deming, the quality guru, wrote about."

"It's similar," commented Jorge. "Six Sigma applies Define-Measure-Analyze-Improve-Control to projects." This DMAIC methodology follows the same pattern as Plan-Do-Check-Act; however, each phase relates to the type of information you would be gathering during that phase. In our class, we're using a roadmap or process map that guides us through each phase. We follow it to help us understand, analyze, and then solve problems in our processes."

Lunch arrived and, as always, Jorge was amazed at how much food Hank could consume. "Where do you put all that food?" he asked incredulously. "If I ate as much as you do, I'd be over 300 pounds in no time!"

"The key, my friend, is exercise," Hank replied, "I run for an hour four mornings a week and lift weights the three other mornings. If you think about it, with 15 useful hours in a day, that's only about 6.7% of my week. For so little effort, I receive a lot of benefits. I can still beat the boys in basketball, and I seem to have more energy. Laura and I have even been swing dancing on Saturday nights, which keeps the romance alive."

Jorge thought for a moment about Laura. She was the first woman whom Hank had dated more than a few times after his divorce. They were good for each other, and Jorge figured that their romance was pretty healthy even without the dancing.

"You know, I've tried to stick with a daily exercise regimen, but I just can't seem to stay committed," lamented Jorge.

"Consistency is the key; you have to keep at it," urged Hank.

"That's funny," Jorge laughed. "Our Six Sigma classes are teaching the same basic ideas: reduce variation and stick to the roadmap."

"So, speaking of consistency, do you think I should create a histogram for both distance and direction for all my clubs?" asked Hank, thinking about the consistency and reduced variation arguments.

"Actually," Jorge said, "you probably already have. For example, I would estimate that your 160-yard 7 iron has a standard deviation of five or six yards. With these estimates you should plan accordingly. Don't depend on hitting your personal best shot, or even your average shot, when picking your club."

***

After Hank devoured his large lunch, the conversation turned back to Six Sigma. "So, you were talking about creating a Six Sigma infrastructure," prompted Hank.

"Creating a successful Six Sigma infrastructure is part of the Define phase and is critical for Six Sigma to be successful. Managers need to develop a clear high-level view of their business so they can identify what areas provide the greatest opportunity for improvement. This is where the *Satellite-Level* metric strategy that I told you about comes in. This methodology is useful for tracking and improving balanced scorecard metrics," replied Jorge.

"We found it really helpful to bring in a Six Sigma consultant to help with the project selection process. There are critical parameters that you look for in initial projects in order to help assure success." Jorge wrote the following project parameters on a napkin for Hank:

- Project is important to the business's success
- Project will have a visible impact
- Project is properly scoped so that the team does not become overwhelmed
- Project should be completed within six months (longer projects can be tackled later after Black Belts have gained more experience)
- Data is available to support the project

"This is also where you can define time-related business metrics that can be used to monitor how the business is

84

doing. Using the right metrics lets you quantify the impact of projects on the business," Jorge explained.

"My wife and I were at a charity benefit last night," Jorge continued. "Six Sigma was mentioned at our table, and it turned out that many of those we talked to were from companies that are implementing Six Sigma. As you might expect, it became obvious during our discussions that companies were experiencing different amounts of success with Six Sigma. Some companies have not had the kind of executive support from their CEO that we are experiencing and it seems that they've been less successful. One measure of how well a CEO is committed is whether Six Sigma is listed within the company's annual report to stockholders, along with its overall benefits and example project benefits. I'm glad Janet, our CEO, is supporting the implementation and using the tools."

"Also, it was obvious that some of these companies weren't asking the right questions or using the best metrics, and their results suffered. For example, some companies were spending a lot of resources counting defects. They were trying to create a defect metric they could use for their entire company. They wanted to calculate an overall sigma quality level in every area of their business. Using this metric, an organization with a defect rate of 3.4 parts per million opportunities is said to be operating at a six sigma quality level. A three sigma quality level is about 67,000 ppm. A four sigma quality level is about 6000 ppm while a five sigma quality level is about 250 ppm."

"Some companies try to use this metric as a primary driver for their Six Sigma implementation, and, while it sounds like a utopian metric, it has major problems. To use it, you have to define opportunities for failure for all activities within your company. This is not only a huge undertaking, but there can be discrepancies on how things are counted. Take your business, for example. What would you consider to be an opportunity for a defect on one of your printed circuit boards?"

Hank thought for a minute and answered, "When manufacturing circuit boards, we could have material problems, assembly problems, handling damage, ..."

Jorge interrupted, "Yeah, but what are the specific opportunities for defects? For example, what type of material problems?"

"Unfortunately, there are many. You could have components that are out of tolerance or broken. You could also have a cracked board. And then there are the assembly problems such as solder bridging, unsoldered joints, reversed parts, missing parts, even wrong parts."

Jorge replied, "From what I've learned in Six Sigma training, there's a standard approach for this situation. You don't count every way a component can have a problem. Instead, each component is counted as one opportunity, with multiple defect types. With this method, the total number of opportunities is obtained by adding the number of components and solder joints."

Jorge continued, "Let's approximate the sigma quality level of your printed circuit board manufacturing lines. How many components would there be per board?"

Hank chewed his fingernail, took a minute to silently count, and responded, "I'd say 300-400 for the Mach II line".

"About how many solder connections would you have?"

"About 600 to 800," Hank responded.

"Okay, let's say the total number of solder joints and components is 1000. How many boards would you make in a typical week? And also, how many defects would you expect?" Jorge asked as he jotted the numbers down on the napkin under the list of project parameters.

"We've been running about 5000 a week and our yield is around 98%," Hank responded immediately.

"Your yield is running about 98%, but how many defects were really created? There could be more than one defect on a board. Also, there could be defects repaired but not counted against the yield. What would you guess defects would be if they were all counted?"

Hank wavered and finally responded, "Well, I'm not certain, but we once did an engineering study on that line, indicating 1250 defects per week. I believe that included all the uncounted touchups and reworks."

"Okay," Jorge said, working the numbers on a new napkin. "For one week you have 5000 boards and each board has 1000 opportunities for defects. That's 5,000,000 opportunities for defects per week. If you divide 1250 defects by 5,000,000, you would have a 250 DPMO rate, which is about a five sigma quality level."

Hank responded, "That's pretty good. With just a little effort I could be at a six sigma quality level!"

"Not so fast, sigma boy. For one thing, you are operating at a 250 DPMO rate or a five sigma quality level. The sigma quality-level metric is not linear. Each incremental improvement is harder than the one before. You would have to make significant process changes to operate at a 3.4 DPMO rate."

Jorge continued, "Secondly, consider the average number of defects you have per board. You have 1250 defects for the 5000 boards you make per week. That could be viewed as an average rework rate of 25%. Doesn't sound so good to me. Looks like you have what we learned in our Six Sigma training as 'hidden factory'. You're doing a lot of rework that is hidden and isn't showing up in your yield numbers."

"So you can see how the sigma quality level metric and even the final yield number are sometimes deceiving," Jorge elaborated and paused to let Hank take it all in. His wheels were obviously spinning.

"Let's step back a second and ask yourself why you have these measures," Jorge spoke, breaking Hank's thought stream.

Hank responded, "We use them as part of our cost of operations. We want to see if we are improving or not. We also want to keep customers happy by delivering good products."

Jorge then replied, "Okay, let's talk costs. Shouldn't you be counting all reworks in your cost calculations? If you're only focusing on final yield numbers, you're missing the cost impact of all those reworks. In Six Sigma terms, we refer to this as the Cost of Poor Quality (COPQ) or the Cost of Doing Nothing Different. This number paints a better picture of what's really happening in your operation. Rather than patting yourself on the back for having a 98% yield or quoting a five sigma quality level, you track the comprehensive DPMO rate over time and convert that to COPQ."

"By doing it this way, you have the true cost. In addition, details of the hidden factory defects can be compiled and used to determine where to focus improvements and subsequently reduce costs."

Hank sat silently with a perplexed frown. He folded up the two napkins carefully and placed them in his worn billfold. After a few minutes, Jorge grew uneasy with the silence, asking his friend if he had rambled too much.

"No, everything makes perfect sense. I'm just wondering how much 98% yield is actually costing the business. First thing on Monday, I'm going to have someone get me the numbers," Hank resolved.

Jorge added, "Well, you've got the idea, but there are a few more areas in which the sigma quality level can be deceiving. I'll give your brain a rest and explain those another time."

Hank beat Jorge to the bill when it arrived. Jorge protested that Hank had won on the last hole, but Hank just smiled and said that this was the most cost-effective business lunch he had ever had. It not only helped him fix his golf game; it had given him a new perspective on his attempts to improve his business. Jorge settled for a chance to buy Hank a beer in the bar.

Hank was hungry for more details, relentless in his search for ways to work more efficiently, and asked, "Jorge, you've talked a lot about training. What does that entail?"

"Technically, I didn't need to attend the Black Belt training. The four week-long sessions over four months really cut into my schedule, but I knew I could do a better job leading the implementation if I was familiar with the details of Six Sigma."

"The first week focused on the measure phase of DMAIC. This is common within many Six Sigma training sessions; however, I've heard that the topics covered within this phase and how it is done can be quite different depending upon the Six Sigma training provider."

"In our training, the measure phase had two components: creating baseline metrics and gathering the Wisdom of the Organization. During the week, we talked about obtaining the voice of the customer and the high-level metrics necessary to describe the outputs of the current process in a manner that leads to the right activities."

"One of the first things described was the 30,000-Foot-Level control charts[4] that I spoke of earlier. This type of chart can get companies out of the fire-fighting mode."

"You know, Jorge, I don't see any high-level type metrics in our Lean rollout. Don't get me wrong; Lean techniques are helping us make some gains, but we are not getting the high-level view of our operation. Now that I think of it, there has been a lot of confusion and debate over where to focus our efforts initially."

"Hank, you really should look into using these charts to help focus your Lean efforts. The other day, the woman next to me on my flight home was a Lean Champion, similar to a Six Sigma Black Belt. She told me that one of the first projects their Lean Consultant had them do was reduce finished goods inventory to almost nothing. Predictably, as soon as their inventory went down, a big order came in. They were forced to spend a lot of money in overtime and expediting shipments."

"When I told her about how we're learning to use a *Satellite-Level* view strategy for our various processes, manufacturing as well as transactional, she told me that they would never have chosen some of their projects if they had considered this type of high-level view of their operations."

"Then we talked about how the project might have gone if they had followed the Six Sigma roadmap I was taught in training. We sketched a rough plan out for her which considered the demand pattern and cycle time of the system and then determined what the finished goods inventory level should have been."

"If you saved all the napkins from all of your Six Sigma discussions, you could give your own training class," Hank acknowledged with a smile. "So far, we've been focusing on improving our cycle times. This may not be a completely fair statement, but it seems after making some improvements, we generate defects faster now! What I am really interested in, after our talk, is how are we impacting the bottom-line?"

"So, let's talk about your Mach II product line," Jorge said. "What do you think is the biggest problem area?"

Hank said, "We're having problems with both defects and cycle times."

"Which is costing you the most money? Don't forget customer dissatisfaction costs money, too."

Hank responded, "Based on our previous conversations, I think that defects are our biggest problem. Our on-time delivery record is not really that bad."

Jorge pulled a stack of napkins from the bar, rolled up his sleeves, and with a proud smile, said, "So let's start outlining a Six Sigma project for you to reduce defects in your Mach II product line." Jorge was eager to strategize, but his mechanical pencil was out of lead. He bummed a pen from the bartender and asked, "How do you currently address defects in production?"

"Well," Hank responded, "we set a criterion for the number of allowable defective units per day. When we exceed those targets, we take corrective action."

"Does your production process exceed this criterion often?" Jorge inquired.

"Unfortunately, yes," Hank responded.

"I would bet that if you tracked these defects on a 30,000-Foot-Level control chart, you'd find you're doing a lot of fire-fighting. In class, the instructor would say that you are attacking common cause variability as though it were special cause. When you're fire-fighting, you're not improving the process and could even make it worse. If you send me some numbers, I'll look at them and make some suggestions." Jorge responded. "If your process has only common cause variability, we would need to examine your data collectively to determine the capability of your process. If the results are not satisfactory, you'll need to work on the overall process. This overall output of a process can be called a key process output variable or KPOV."

"Geeze," Hank said pensively. "Yesterday I really laid into the plant manger at our San Francisco facility for not meeting his monthly targets. I then asked the manager to determine what happened during the last measurement period, forcing him into the fire-fighting mode, I'm sure, which will probably lead to more inefficient actions."

Hank whacked himself playfully on the forehead. "I asked the wrong question. I bet a lot of my managers fire-fight events that stem from common cause variability. We should be focusing on data over a longer period of time, to get a picture of the process, and then analyze what we need to do differently to improve."

"Exactly," Jorge responded, excited that his paper napkin class was beginning to sink into Hank's thinking.

Hank, inspired that things were beginning to make sense, continued, "The implications of this metric could be huge. We could apply this approach to many other areas of the business, including sales and service. Taking a high-level view of our strategic processes over time could help us reduce the amount of daily fire-fighting, creating a view of our entire organization as a system. Then, we could proactively drill down with strategic Six Sigma projects that really impact the bottom line."

After shoveling a handful of pretzels into his mouth and washing it down with ice water, Hank asked, "Did you read The *Fifth Discipline* by Peter Senge[5]?"

Jorge hadn't, so Hank explained, "He talks about a learning organization. If implemented wisely, we can use these metrics and other tools within Six Sigma to help our organization become a learning organization. We would become curious about our processes, embrace change, and gain confidence with each successful improvement. This could transform our organization and increase growth, which is really what is important to our shareholders."

Jorge stole the pretzel bowl away from Hank before Hank devoured them all. Now he was starving. He looked down at his watch, surprised to find that it was already time for dinner. Time just flew whenever he started talking about Six Sigma. Maybe he should consider becoming a full-time instructor.

***

As the sun began to set on the golf course, Jorge and Hank decided to stay and have dinner on the patio of the

93

clubhouse, enjoying the sunset and finishing their discussion of Six Sigma.

Once they had ordered, Jorge continued, "Our instructor stressed that organizations achieving success with Six Sigma learn to apply the most appropriate tool or measure for each process. There is no one-size-fits-all metric or tool appropriate for all processes."

"Hmmm... sort of like learning that changing to a 3 iron off the tee is not the answer for everyone, you are saying that Six Sigma offers some useful metrics that could be beneficial to a particular process but not necessarily to all processes," Hank reiterated.

"As I mentioned earlier, DPMO is a metric that some organizations try to force onto every process, but it's not always easy to describe what an opportunity is for every process." Jorge fished around for something to sketch on, but the napkins were cloth, causing them both to chuckle.

Improvising, Jorge pulled a receipt from his billfold and illustrated an example for defects on a piece of sheet metal. A natural teacher, as he drew he lectured, "You could describe a defect opportunity as one square inch, one square foot, or one square millimeter. You can see the confusion that could arise with multiple definitions for opportunities. In transactional processes, this practice gets even crazier. However, as we talked about before, DPMO does have its uses."

Hank hungrily picked up the receipt, folded it carefully, and placed it in his billfold next to the napkins from lunch, as Jorge continued, "Another Six Sigma metric, which may or may not be useful, is Rolled Throughput Yield (RTY). This metric can be useful to describe the hidden factory we talked about earlier. It is calculated by multiplying together the yields for each step of the process. This can highlight the amount of rework within a process and where it is occurring. However, this metric can require a lot of work to generate and is not appropriate for all situations."

The waiter brought their dinner, and they each ordered an Irish beer with their meal, which was inspired by Jorge's recent trip with Sandra to Ireland. They took a break from their informal Six Sigma class and devoured the battered deep-fried fish and salty fries, Hank shared the highlights of their week-long bicycling tour, mostly detailing the pubs and the people of Ireland.

After dinner, the waiter delivered coffee and the paper napkins Hank had requested. Jorge continued his lecture but warned Hank that he would have to wrap things up soon and get home. "So, after you decide upon your primary 30,000-Foot-Level metric, you then assess whether your process is in control and has the capability to deliver a desirable output. If the process is not capable of meeting customer requirements, next you would tap the Wisdom of the Organization via people who know the process intimately. The end goal is to solicit improvement ideas using brainstorming tools such as cause-and-effect diagrams."

Hank, intrigued but confused, asked, "Can you give me an actual example?"

"Let me go through a project we are working on to illustrate some of the ideas we have been talking about. It's a transactional project dealing with Days Sales Outstanding or DSO. To create this metric, we randomly selected one invoice daily and then determined when the payment was received relative to the due date. If it was a day early, we would record a -1 for the KPOV, in this case, DSO. If it was a day late, we would record a +1 for the KPOV. Then we control-charted DSO at the 30,000-Foot-Level," Jorge explained while sketching a control chart.

"At first, we thought we should have more frequent sampling, not just one point for each day. However, the instructor encouraged us to use the reduced sampling to get a summary of our common cause variability inherent to DSO. Only after analyzing these numbers would we know *if* a need existed to drill down further. Wisdom of the Organization would then guide us as to *where* to drill down. This early assessment of where we needed to focus saved us a lot of time and money by not collecting data in areas that weren't major problems," Jorge explained with satisfaction.

"After we've examined data over a relatively long period of time, the question became 'How are we doing relative to the needs of our customers?' We then used process capability techniques to estimate the percentage of times we failed to meet customer needs." Jorge spoke easily as he sketched and explained a probability plot that he drew under the control chart, carefully plotting out example data points.

After finishing the sketch, Jorge continued, "We also calculated the cost of not receiving payment by the due date. An interesting part of this project is that we learned to convert the DSO from a pass-fail attribute response to a numeric response."

"The advantage of using a numeric response is that if we set up a criterion of 60 days, a payment of 61 days is not weighted the same as a payment of 120 days."

The light bulb in Hank's head flashed on, and he commented, "You know, airlines should do something like this. If a flight leaves within 15 minutes of scheduled departure, it's considered on time. This means a flight that is three hours late is no more late than one that is 16 minutes late. From a customer point of view, that doesn't make sense."

Jorge said, "You're right. This re-emphasizes that we need to have metrics that encourage the right activities. If a flight is 16 minutes late, why should the crew rush since they have already been given a failure check mark for being late for that particular flight departure?"

Hank leaned back a moment and smiled, "And it's sort of like one of my putts that misses the hole by a few inches, compared to one that misses by a few feet. They are both defects, but the first one only costs me one stroke, while the second may cost more."

The golf comment made Jorge think of Wayne and Zack. "One of the defects that caused Zack to miss today's game was transaction errors, another type of problem you might assign a Six Sigma team to tackle. The scope of the project might be to improve the transaction entry process in order to reduce the number of transaction errors at a single office."

Jorge continued, "For this situation, the number of transaction errors would be the KPOV. Remember that the KPOV is important because it can tell you whether the customer is going to be satisfied. Notice, however, that this measurement comes too late in the process to avoid waste or an unsatisfied customer."

Hank handed him another napkin as Jorge calculated Zack's example.

"So, in Zack's case, if there are 2.5 transaction errors per 1000 one month, and 4.8 per 1000 the next, how do you know if the transaction entry process has changed for the worse?" Jorge asked.

"What kind of question is that? Of course it's getting worse," Hank responded without thinking.

"It seems like it is getting worse, but you can't really tell until you compare it to the normal range of the process. In the class we used 30,000-Foot-Level control charts to establish this range of common cause variability. If a 30,000-Foot-Level control chart had limits of 1.75 to 6.0 errors per 1000 transactions, then there is no evidence to indicate that the process has changed for the months with 2.5 and 4.8 errors per 1000 transactions," Jorge turned teacher again. "The 30,000-Foot-Level control chart is useful to baseline our process. A baseline is important here because it answers questions about when process changes occur."

Hank thought about improving his golf game again. "So I should keep 30,000-Foot-Level control charts on my golf scores, maybe even the number of fairways and greens hit, and number of putts per round **just** so I'll know when I need to practice a particular part of my game?"

Jorge nodded and said, "Exactly. And you could also use them to see if your practice was working."

Shifting gears, he continued, "Up until now we've been talking about the measure phase. The next step of the DMAIC process is the analyze phase. The key to solving problems is to find what step within the process is driving the KPOVs. Key Process Input Variables or KPIVs influence the KPOVs. In Zack's case, the KPIVs may be the number of transactions a clerk has to handle hourly or the method of entering transactions into the computer. So the measure phase is focused on developing a baseline for the KPOVs and collecting organizational wisdom on what the KPIVs might be. To do this we would use tools such as cause-and-effect diagrams, cause-and-effect matrices, and Failure Mode and Effects Analyses, or FMEA."

"Then, in the analyze phase, we test hypothesized cause-and-effect relationships to see if there is statistical significance. Areas found significant can lead us to new insights about where we should focus our improvement efforts."

Hank was really excited. He saw the possibilities of this methodology. This would allow him to restructure the implementation of his Lean program to focus on bottom line issues. He could use this approach to attack the loss of market share! After all, that was a KPOV. Surely there had to be some KPIVs that he could use to improve market share.

The waiter interrupted Jorge's class and placed the bill on the table. Hank quickly grabbed it again. "I'll get this one, Jorge; it is the least I can do for the time you have spent with me today. I know you have a lot of other things going on right now, plus I need room in my wallet for the rest of the class," Hank stated gratefully.

"Thank you, Hank, but it has really been my pleasure. Let's wrap this class up and we will talk more on another day, probably the next golf outing. Since you are now an advanced student, you can help me inform the others," Jorge said jokingly.

Chapter 8: Turning Point

Don't Relax... Be Ready

If you try real hard to relax, you will become either very tense or else so limp you might fall over.

I prefer to put it this way: Be at ease. If you feel at ease, you are relaxed-but ready.

Harvey Penick's Little Red Book

September

A few days before their September golf date, Jorge called Hank. "I realized that I had not talked to you about the voice of the customer. This is critical to everything else you do with Six Sigma. Unless you understand what the customers want or need, you can't tell how **they** think you're doing. Haven't you been frustrated at times about poor service? Could it be that the provider doesn't know what you want?"

Hank responded, "I sure have. For example, they keep putting these surveys on the golf carts asking for our evaluation of the golf course. Seems like they ask the wrong questions. At the bottom I sometimes write my comments, but nothing changes. I think that it's not too much to ask that they offer a decaffeinated soft drink on the refreshment golf cart. I have mentioned it several times on the form as well as to the person driving the cart."

"Exactly," Jorge responded. "What good are surveys if nobody reads them or ever takes action? Important feedback goes to some front-line employee and never gets to someone who can make a difference. Within Six Sigma, we want to create processes that give us the true voice of the customer and use it to help drive our internal improvements."

***

Hank was excited to be on his way to the golf course to meet the guys. He had met with Jorge's Six Sigma provider, and things were progressing well. His managers had begun to define strategic goals and associated processes. They had also assigned the job of understanding customer needs to some key employees in the marketing department. Yesterday, strategic project areas were identified in new product development, warehousing, and shipping. But Hank was most excited about the specific project of which he was Champion: reducing manufacturing cycle time for their Mach II product line. He practically had the entire project on Jorge's paper napkins completed, and it tied in nicely with his company's current Lean activities.

The management team decided to imbed the Lean philosophy and tools into the Six Sigma Business Strategy. They planned to use the high-level Six Sigma metrics to help with the selection of tools, Lean or Six Sigma.

In his almost ten years with Hi-Tech, this was the first time Hank had seen the connection between the overall business strategies and planned improvement projects. He felt more confident now than when they were implementing Lean without Six Sigma. The estimated savings were calculated in the millions the first year, which would more than pay for the training and consulting investments.

**

As Hank pulled into the parking lot, he saw the others congregated around Jorge's SUV. Jorge was sitting on the back bumper with the hatch open, changing shoes.

"Good morning," Hank called out to the group as he lifted his bag from the trunk of his red convertible.

Jorge and Wayne replied, but Zack seemed preoccupied. Zack had showed up to play golf, but he was having a tough time concentrating. The CEO at Z-Credit Financial had reorganized the company and moved him to VP of Operations of a smaller firm they had recently purchased. Zack was especially upset that the CEO had brought in his latest whiz kid to turn things around within Zack's former group. It had all happened over two weeks before, but Zack was still upset and couldn't make sense of how things had gotten so bad.

"What's wrong, Zack?" Hank asked, not quite expecting the answer he received.

"We had a reorganization. They reassigned me to VP of Operations for some little company we just bought. Technically, it was a lateral move, but it sure feels like a demotion. I think our CEO wasn't happy with my performance so he put me in this company that can't be screwed up any more than it already is. My replacement is a whiz kid from Harvard who used to report to me and is my son's age. I start my new job as soon as 'wonder boy' gets back from in a two weeks."

"I'm sorry to hear that, Zack," Jorge sympathized.

"This offers you a great opportunity to take a nothing company and turn it around," Wayne offered, in an attempt to lift Zack's spirits.

Zack responded, "How can I turn around a company that is in the dumps when I couldn't run a company that had a solid performance history?"

Hank was about to jump in and tell him all the news about Six Sigma, but before he could get started Jorge said, "Hey, let's play. We can talk about this later. Right now, I'm going to teach you guys a thing or two about golf."

Sensing Zack's distress, Jorge decided to change the game in an attempt to avoid a total meltdown. At the first tee, Jorge said, "Let's change things today. Let's play a two-man scramble. Each player hits his shot, and then each team selects the best of their two shots and both partners play their next stroke from there. We can keep the same teams so that each side has a long-ball hitter and a short-game player. It should be fun for a change. The team with the lowest total score wins. Same bet?"

Everyone agreed, although no one's heart really seemed to be in it. They played four holes before anyone mentioned work, a course record. By that time, Zack really needed to vent and said, "I don't understand what happened. The Baldrige Assessment was going well. We were identifying areas to work on, making some process improvements, but we really didn't see any tangible results."

Wayne commiserated, attempting to ease Zack's nerves, "You know, we have been having some success as well, but our TQM program hasn't been what I expected. We now have a whole TQM group, and they have to interact with our management team. It seems like there are always disagreements and misunderstandings. The TQM group doesn't seem to understand the pressure on the production managers to meet their schedules and quotas. In turn, the production managers are always complaining that the TQM projects shut their lines down to fix problems that don't really affect production. It seems like the only projects we're having success with are the cross-functional ones in which the process owner is truly championing the project."

"That's it!" cried Hank as he totally missed his tee shot, which went about 60 yards, but he didn't seem to mind the distraction or the bad shot. "That's one of the key differences between Six Sigma and TQM. With Six Sigma, the people responsible for the process are responsible for improving it. You can't achieve success with a separate group to fix problems. There is no buy-in."

"When did you become an expert on Six Sigma?" probed Wayne.

"I wasn't, until last month, when you two," Hank said sarcastically while pointing his driver at Wayne and Zack, "were too busy working to join us. Jorge explained Six Sigma to me, and a light went on. You boys missed an interesting discussion. "

Wayne asked, "Jorge must have said something really good to get you off the Lean bandwagon. What did he say?"

"I'll lay it out for you at lunch," Hank responded. " I still have all my notes."

Out on the fairway, Hank and Jorge made the easy decision to play Jorge's drive. It was a typical Jorge shot of modest length and a slight fade. But it was on the fairway, and the green was reachable. It was far better than

Hank's distracted effort. Hank said about it, "I guess that was really an outlier on my driver control chart." Jorge agreed that there probably was a real special cause this time: the distraction during his swing. From their position on the fairway, Jorge hit a decent fairway wood to the front edge of the green, and then Hank hit a magnificent 4 iron to the center of the green. This team stuff in a scramble has its benefits, both thought as they moved on.

Meanwhile, Wayne had hit another typical drive, long and straight in the middle of the fairway, making Zack's wild hook of no consequence. Hank thought briefly, my maximum distance is better than Wayne's, but his distance and directional variation are less than half of mine. I should benchmark his driving process.

Wayne and Zack both hit their second shots, with short irons, from where Wayne's drive had landed. When they reached the green, they were farther away and putted first. Zack looked over the 18-footer, and putted first. Zack saw the break and his read was perfect, but his stroke was a bit strong. His ball rimmed out of the cup and spun about two feet past the cup.

"Good read, partner… good putt," said Wayne. He had been standing directly behind Zack on line with the hole during his putt. He had not seen the subtle break at the end of the putt, but, armed with knowledge, he stepped up and sweetly stroked the 18-footer into the back of the cup.

"Great putt," exclaimed Zack. "Way to go, partner."

"It was easy once you showed me the line," said Wayne. "How did you know it would break at the end like that?"

Zack was confused, "What do you mean? I just looked at it and could see the break at the end. Also, I could see the grain was against us, so it would be a little slower and break a bit more. All I did was look at it. That's all I ever do."

"Me too," said Wayne, "but I certainly didn't see that little break or the grain." Suddenly it struck him. "You know, I've been having some trouble finding my ball when it is not on the fairway, too. Karen is right! Maybe I do need to get my eyes checked."

Hank chimed in, "You know, they say that Tiger was seeing the breaks in the green better after he got that laser eye surgery. It was right before he started that incredible run of victories. I think they can even make corrections for you guys with bifocals."

"Of course," Wayne nodded. "My problem wasn't a bad putter at all. It was a bad read because I couldn't see the subtle changes in the green. Zack, you've made my day. Thanks, partner."

Zack began to feel better, and appreciated any affirmation from a golfer of Wayne's caliber. Besides, with Zack's reading and Wayne's putting, they easily won the scramble!

***

During lunch, Hank elaborated, with help from Jorge, on the insights he had recently gained from Six Sigma. He explained how Jorge had analyzed some of his data and showed that there was a common cause problem that should be addressed head-on with a Six Sigma project. After Hank and Jorge split the bill, they all walked together towards their cars.

Zack asked, "OK, I think I get it, but how does this affect my business?"

Ignoring Zack's question, Wayne interrupted, "You were making a point about TQM earlier. Could you finish that?"

Jorge was glad to see that his friends were interested. He knew how exciting it could be to understand how powerful the Six Sigma methodology really was.

"As I was saying," Hank stated proudly, "TQM tends to be driven by the Quality Department, whereas Six Sigma is driven by the entire management team. Projects are orchestrated across functions. Our Six Sigma training for management and employees is going to change how they do their jobs. Hank continued, "For the first time, I feel like we have control over our business. Well, control is probably too strong a word, but we understand where our problems are and have a roadmap to eliminate them. This applies to all areas of the business from marketing to manufacturing to customer service. So, Zack, when you said you inherited a loser, that just makes your opportunities that much greater. You'll be able to make big improvements quickly, and you'll be the hero."

Hank continued, "There are people who do great things with their organizations. The problem is that the gains can't be maintained when the person leaves. Results are dependent on the person. That is why I used to reorganize so often. I was looking for those special people. With Six Sigma, getting results has been systematized. The key is to find executives and managers who can execute the Six Sigma business strategy. They don't have to be super heroes; after all, there are only so many of those."

As they reached his SUV, Jorge said, "Well, here we are again. Another good day on the golf course in the record books. Tell you what. Now that you are all up to speed on what I have been doing up till last month, I'll treat you to breakfast tomorrow and elaborate on my more recent events."

"Wow, we can hardly wait," Wayne, Zack, and Hank echoed.

Chapter 9: Improvement

Practicing the Full Swing

Choose a 7 iron or a 6 iron, whichever one you feel the most confidence in, and use it for 80 percent of all your full-swing practice.

The best way to learn to trust your swing is by practicing your swing with a club you trust.

Harvey Penick's Little Red Book

Breakfast the next day

They all knew what they wanted to order for breakfast the next morning, so Jorge jumped right in. "As Hank and I described earlier, within the analyze phase we conduct passive analyses to determine the inputs that may impact our Key Process Output Variables or KPOVs. Inputs that affect our outputs are called Key Process Input Variables or KPIVs. In engineering terms we could describe this relationship through the equation $Y=f(x)$. Y would be a KPOV, while x is a KPIV. Teams use Organizational Wisdom to prioritize all the potential inputs and decide which to study further. The Six Sigma tools used here include cause-and-effect diagrams, cause-and-effect matrices, and FMEAs."

"To test the relationship of our perceived KPIVs, our Black Belts use graphical analysis and statistical tools such as multi-vari charts, analysis of variance, and regression analysis. At first, when I reviewed Black Belt projects, I referred frequently to the project execution roadmap from my training manual in order to know what tool was most appropriate. It's a great way to learn about the tools. After only a few times, it became second nature."

"I'm currently reviewing the project we discussed on Days Sales Outstanding or DSO. The Wisdom of the Organization on this project gave us many potential KPIV's. However, there were some low-hanging-fruit issues that could be easily rectified; for example, getting all the billing departments to follow a single procedure."

"When we did this, our 30,000-Foot-Level control chart went out-of-control for the better. We also did some statistical analyses that quantified, with a confidence interval, our potential for long-term improvement."

"What is a confidence interval?" Zack interrupted.

"Confidence intervals are like those reported during elections, when they give a margin of error. Confidence intervals are important because they quantify the uncertainties related to making statements from samples," Jorge explained.

Wayne then interrupted and said, "You know, I think that happened to me the other day. During our TQM implementation, we made a process change that we thought would make an improvement. We felt good when we ran a couple trials, and it looked like there was an improvement. However, I'm not convinced that the process really changed. It seems like the changes we saw were from common variation."

Wayne elaborated, "It is unfortunate that we do not have a 30,000-Foot-Level metric chart as a baseline so we could see what happened over the long haul. The sad point is that we made some very expensive changes to our process and we don't have a clue whether the changes were beneficial or detrimental. By the time we finally are able to tell for sure, we may have spent a lot of money and wasted a lot of time."

"Wayne, you're right on," Hank said. "I think this happens a lot. Without Six Sigma, you can be answering the wrong question. Previously we all had our own biases on what was causing defects in the printed circuit manufacturing process. When we let our prejudices about processes guide us without conducting a statistical analysis, it often led to major cost implications."

Jorge continued, "We followed the Six Sigma roadmap for the DSO metric for our invoicing process. Wisdom of the Organization led us to think that there might be a difference between companies invoiced. Also, we thought that the size of an invoice might make a difference. Our passive statistical analysis showed that the average DSO was significantly different between companies; however, the relationship between the size of the invoice and the DSO was not statistically significant."

Wayne joked.

Jorge responded, "I guess so ... a little bit. I'm getting excited because I'm starting to see people make decisions based on information rather than on sketchy data and gut feel."

Hank then said, "Let me tell you about what happened to us on one of our projects. We used Gage R&R (Repeatability and Reproducibility) to quantify the consistency of the measurement system in one of our projects. It's an area we often overlook, and we were extremely surprised by the results. Almost 40% of our total process variability was due to measurement variation. With the existing gage, we were accepting bad parts and rejecting good parts. When we included the cost of rework, lost production, and replacing customer shipments, we calculated that this gage alone was costing us five million dollars a year. We never would have found this without a structured Six Sigma methodology. We just assumed that as long as the gage was calibrated everything was okay. We never realized that calibration of the measurement system was only one part of the equation."

Wayne interrupted, "That is sort of like my eyes. They were not capable of measuring the break or the speed of a putt, so I was missing them in all directions. All of the money I wasted on new putters pales in comparison to the money I've lost to you guys because I couldn't see the line on the putting green. You will all be happy to know that I have an eye appointment next week, and I should be making a lot more putts soon."

Everyone groaned, but Hank thought about resurrecting his idea of sponsoring Wayne on the senior tour as an investment opportunity.

"Do you remember a couple months ago when I was having problems with transactional errors?" Zack asked.

Jorge laughingly responded, "Your ears must have been burning last week. Hank and I had a long discussion on how we thought your situation lends itself directly to Six Sigma."

Zack responded, "If I could make some low-hanging-fruit improvements, I might get my job back or at least leave with some scrap of dignity... if I can make some quick improvements. What wisdom on the green did I miss?"

For the next few minutes, Hank and Jorge filled Zack in on the particulars of the conversation they had had last month. They agreed to look at some of Zack's data and help him outline a strategy.

As they got up to leave the breakfast table, Jorge looked at Zack and offered, "Now that we have helped with Wayne's golf game, would you like a suggestion?"

Zack felt like he was on a roll here and responded, "Sure, shoot!"

"Well, Wayne's problem was not his putter, but his vision. Hank's problem was one of course management, that is making smarter club selections based not just on his best ever shot, but on the expected variation with different clubs."

"OK, but what about me?" Zack asked impatiently.

"Your problem is different. It's not any particular club, and it's certainly not physical. Your eyes are great, and your physique is good, too. Your problem is more basic," Jorge said. "Your problem is very fundamental. Your grip, your alignment, even your swing are all too much like your old baseball-playing days. As a result, you have processes with too much variation. Hooks, slices, topped shots, thin shots, a little of everything."

"I guess I should just give the game up, then," Zack moaned.

"Not at all," said Jorge. "Actually, it's easy to fix. Just get a little coaching on the fundamentals of the stance, grip, and swing, and practice with your 7 iron until it feels natural. An hour with a pro and a few buckets of balls are all it will take for you to break 90 almost every time."

"But what about all the other clubs? Don't I need a new driver?" Zack questioned.

Jorge finished, "Don't worry about that now. Your problems are so fundamental that you can fix them without much effort. The 7 iron is the easiest to hit and will help you ingrain the fundamental changes quickly. Only then can you tell whether you really need to make any adjustments to your equipment. My guess is you won't need to make any."

"Wow," said Zack, "with all the help you're giving me in my business and my golf game, I'll have enough time to salvage my family life, too!"

Chapter 10: Enlightenment

The Chip Shot

The first and foremost fundamental to learn about chipping is this: keep your hands ahead of or even with the clubhead on the follow through. All the way through.

Always Chip the ball if:
1. *The lie is poor.*
2. *The green is hard.*
3. *You have a downhill lie.*
4. *The wind has an influence on the shot.*
5. *You are under stress.*

Harvey Penick's Little Red Book

October

With paper in hand, Jorge approached the boys on their way to the practice green. Excitedly, he called out, "Zack, we were right about your data. It appears to be a common cause problem. A 30,000-Foot-Level control chart of your transactional errors indicates that your process is not changing. The up and down variation of the data is from the noise within your process. From the criteria that you sent me, I expect that you are fire-fighting about 10% of the time."

Zack said, "Hey, that seems right because we spend about two days a month chasing transactional entry errors that have error rates beyond our criterion. Let me see the chart."

Jorge gave Zack the printout and said, "The charts show you haven't really fixed anything. How much do you think that is costing your business?"

Zack shook his head in disbelief and then replied, "You sure know how to use data to hurt a guy's feelings. I don't have a clue how much this is costing the business, but I know it's not pretty!"

Hank suggested, "Zack, if you want to reduce the error rate, you could do some passive analyses, like we talked about last week, which might even lead to a DOE."

"DOE?" Zack asked, barely lifting his eyes from the control chart.

"DOE is short for Design of Experiments. I can explain it in more detail after we get some practice putts in. The rain last night probably slowed the greens down," Hank said, eager to play.

Zack had also found some time for a lesson with the pro, and everyone noticed his new swing even in the warm-ups on the first tee. His stance was square, his grip was neutral, and his smooth swing now looked more like Wayne's swing than they could ever have imagined. When Zack teed off, it was 250 yards on the fairway, with just a hint of draw. The others all commented that they might need to adjust handicaps for the group if this continued.

***

Waiting at the second tee, Wayne asked, "Did you finish the DSO project yet, Jorge?"

Jorge replied, "You may remember, our Wisdom of the Organization led us to examine the size of invoice and the customer invoiced. Passive analysis tools from our Six Sigma roadmap led us to a statistically significant issue between customers. That is, the customer invoiced was identified as a key process input variable for DSO."

"We then brainstormed about what we might do differently to improve our DSO response. However, to validate these improvement ideas, we needed to execute some tests, using Design of Experiments, as Hank mentioned earlier."

"We came up with a list of seven factors to evaluate during the DOE. Some of these factors were process noise variables such as from which hospital the invoice originated. We also included things we could change within our process, including billing formats for example. For the experiment, we set up each of the seven factors with two levels. For example, in the case of the factor-billing department there were two locations, 1 and 2. From our passive analyses earlier, we thought location number 1 did better and location number 2 did worse."

"If you consider all combinations of factors and levels, experiments can get to be very large. However, with fractional factorial DOE experimentation we can use a subset of all combinations, and this reduced our number of tests from 128 to 16, while still obtaining very valuable information from our process."

"Oh, you get a free lunch for not having to do 128 trials," Zack remarked sarcastically.

Jorge responded, "Not exactly. When we conduct this type of experiment, we confound information about our interactions; however, this is not all bad since it saves us a lot of time. Before I get to that, I should describe what an interaction is. Remember the old copier machines in the 1970's?"

"That was way before my time," Zack bragged facetiously.

"Sure," Jorge replied dryly, "you're so much younger than the rest of us. Anyway, copier-feed failures were a major problem. Two KPIVs were ambient temperature and humidity. If you compared feed failure rates at 68 and 98 degrees at low humidity, no change was noticeable. However, at high humidity if you compare feed failure rates at either 68 degrees or 98 degrees, a significant change is indicated. Feed failures were higher when both the humidity and the temperature were high. This means that there was interaction between the two factors, temperature and humidity. The real problem source was that the moisture in the air was the highest at this condition, which resulted in water absorption of the paper and feed problems. You cannot understand the effect of these factors without looking at both of them together."

Jorge continued, "If an interaction exists within our process, we may never find the solution by changing one factor at a time. A well-structured DOE manages the confounding of two-factor interactions. Anyway, there is too much detail to get involved with DOE on the golf course. You need much of a week's Black Belt training to understand fully the benefits of DOE and how to plan them efficiently. But, it is a very powerful strategy applicable to many situations."

***

As the match progressed, Jorge realized that everyone was playing better today. He was keeping his shots in play and using his short game to great effect around the greens. At the turn, he was out in 38, and Hank had thought his way to an intelligent 39 with no penalty strokes. Wayne had made several putts with his new glasses for a one-under 35, and Jorge wondered what would happen after the laser surgery that was scheduled in a few days. Even Zack had demonstrated remarkable variation reduction with his new swing and had shot 44 on the front. The match stood even, but Jorge realized they were all 'winning'.

***

Waiting at the turn, Wayne asked, "So are DOE techniques applicable to all projects?"

"Not always," Hank responded. "All Six Sigma tools have applications, and each of them should be used when most appropriate. However, DOE techniques are very beneficial, both to manufacturing and transactional situations."

Hank continued, "It's like in golf, where there are usually several ways to hit a shot. Some are easier to hit than others. Some ways have less variability in their results, like Jorge talks about. Picking the right tool is always important. For our DSO project we conducted a DOE where we considered seven factors. During our passive analysis, we found that there were two group of customers: those making timely payments and those that were chronically late. We treated this as one of our seven factors. Another factor we looked at was whether or not we gave the customer a reminder call a week after invoicing," Jorge added.

As they approached the tenth green, Jorge sliced his approach shot more to the right than normal and ended up behind a tree. When they found the ball, it was about 4 feet directly behind a medium sized tree with a forked trunk and low hanging branches. Wayne and Zack feigned disappointment at Jorge's lot.

"Looks like that tree has you stymied," said Zack with a heavy dose of mock sympathy.

"Yeah, I guess it's up to you on this hole, partner," Jorge said to Hank.

"Maybe not," said Hank as he looked at the shot more carefully.

Jorge was directly behind the tree, and the base of the eight-inch trunk blocked his path to the hole while overhanging branches restricted the shot selection to a height of less than 5 feet. However, Hank noticed that the natural 'V' in the trunk left an opening to the flag that was almost three feet wide at the top and narrowed down to nothing at ground level.

Hank said, "Look at this! You're back far enough that you can chip right through the fork of this tree with your 5 iron. That should keep it down below the branches, but get it up just enough to go through the 'V' in the trunk. Bump it into the face of the green, and it should run right up to the hole. You can still get it up and down!"

Zack and Wayne taunted Jorge as he lined up the shot, but their jeers turned to cheers of amazement as he executed an almost perfect bump and run shot, exactly as instructed.

"Thanks for the 'GET OUT OF JAIL FREE' card, partner. How do you come up with such creative ideas?" Jorge asked with a satisfied grin.

"Good judgement. You know, it comes from experience, and experience comes from bad judgement. My length gets me into a lot of trouble on the course. I've been in so many tough situations that I've learned to be creative. I just used my extensive Organization Wisdom to pick the right tool for the job."

"The best thing about being a teacher is that I learn so much!" Hank said as he punctuated his comment by tapping in his miracle par putt.

As they all moved to the next tee, Jorge continued his discussion, "Through DOE, we discovered that our late customers were paying sooner on average when they received reminder calls a week after they were initially invoiced. The companies that normally pay on time showed no change when they received reminders. This is an example of the kind of interaction we talked about earlier. Because of this objective data, we were able to motivate change in the process. For our new process, we will have a reminder call, one week after invoicing, only for those companies that are historically delinquent. As you can imagine, this will save us a lot of time and money. In addition, our good-paying clients won't get frustrated with our phone calls."

Hank added, "In our circuit board defect-reduction project, the passive analysis tools led us to a significant issue of cleanliness within our printed circuit board manufacturing process. Cleanliness was identified as a KPIV for the defect rate KPOV. We then brainstormed for what we might do differently to improve cleanliness. In order to validate these improvement ideas, we need to perform some tests. That's where we'll be using DOE, like Jorge has been describing."

As the round ended, the match ended up even, but the entire group felt like winners. Everyone had played well, with Wayne shooting par 72, Hank a 79, Jorge 80, and even Zack broke through with an 89. As they drove to the cars to deposit the clubs, Jorge thought that this was not just a random combination of unlikely occurrences. This was more likely an example of real systemic improvement in everyone's game.

***

As they reached his SUV, Jorge suggested, "I hate to bring this up, but this approach could also help Zack improve the effectiveness of a potential project that he has not discussed yet."

"What project is that?" Zack asked.

"Doesn't your financial company send out junk mail to solicit business?" Jorge replied.

Zack tersely responded, "We prefer to view this activity as a mass mailing."

"Given what we've discussed about DOE, don't you think you could use these techniques to improve the response rate from your mass mailings?" Jorge quizzed.

"Maybe it would help and could even improve my standing with our CEO. How would it work exactly?" Zack replied.

Jorge responded, "Well, you would basically follow the process that we did for our projects. When you get to the point of asking yourself what should be done differently, there will probably be differences of opinion. Let's consider that one idea was sending a very large post card instead of an envelope for your mass mailings. This would be cheaper than sending a letter and might stand out better against all the other junk mail."

"Mass mail," Zack corrected.

"Anyway," Jorge started laughing, "before you change to this new marketing strategy, you'd want to test its effectiveness."

"Hey, Jorge," Wayne interrupted, "why don't you install an overhead projector in this SUV so you can show slides when we have class out here in the parking lot?"

Jorge ignored the laughter and continued, "With a traditional approach, we would send out trial post cards and compare the number of responses we get to what we had previously. This approach can cause problems. There is a time delay between the change and response. Also, something else could have happened in the economy that affected our response. That would be considered a confounding effect. To compare the envelope mailing with the post card approach, we would have to send out some envelopes and some post cards during the same time frame."

"That would be easy to do and give us valuable information on our process," Zack agreed.

Jorge responded, "Great. We could do this and then compare the responses statistically. However, I believe that there might be other factors that should be considered at the same time, such as time of the month that the mailing goes out, your mailing list source, and maybe if the recipient is male or female?"

Zack then said, "All of these factors could make a difference."

Jorge responded, "If that's the case, they all should be considered within the DOE."

Zack asked, "But won't that mix things up?"

"Not if the experiment is conducted correctly. When you get back to the office, give me a call. I'll show you a reference that illustrates this point vividly," Jorge responded.

Wayne jumped in, stating, "You know I think that DOE could help within our product development process."

Jorge responded, "That's right. Within Design for Six Sigma or DFSS, DOEs can be very beneficial. You could use a DOE to evaluate structurally various combinations of input conditions that might affect a response. You could assess these factors in a structured way, combining manufacturing conditions with customer applications. This would help you select the best combination of factor settings to give the best results for your customers. You can also use DOE techniques to develop a test strategy for new products. When I get back to the office, I'll also give you a reference example from our Six Sigma textbook that illustrates how DOE can be useful in development organizations. The bottom line is: Whenever you are considering testing something, consider DOE."

Zack then said, "Sounds like DOE can be very beneficial."

Jorge then said, "Not to change the subject, but I was thinking about what Hank said last month about Gage R&R. We're not currently taking this on as a project; however, many of the tests within hospitals are executed and interpreted as though there are no testing errors. This is especially alarming when we state that tests for AIDS are either positive or negative. In either case, if we are wrong the consequences to the patients and their families can be devastating."

Hank responded. "I think that all industries should be more sensitive to Gage R&R and measurement error. When measurement variation is unsatisfactory, we can make wrong decisions. For example, our court system is a measurement system for evaluating guilt. And, it's subject to errors. Now with DNA testing, that measurement system has improved."

Wayne said, "You've sold me. I'm going to set up a meeting with our CEO to discuss how we'll roll out Six Sigma."

With that, four happy and relaxed golfers headed home with hopes for continued improvement.

Chapter 11: Making Progress

The Pitch Shot

Probably you want to pitch the ball if:
1. *The lie is good.*
2. *You have an uphill lie.*
3. *The green is very soft.*
4. *There is an obstacle in the way.*

Harvey Penick's Little Red Book

November

It was a beautiful November day, nice enough that Zack had the top down on his convertible as he pulled into the course parking lot. Today he was looking good and feeling good.

The first thing out of Zack's mouth when he saw Hank at the practice green was, "I expected to see you at the driving range. Are you taking Jorge's advice and practicing your weaknesses instead of your strengths?" When Hank just smiled and ignored him, he tried, "From the Six Sigma book you recommended on the phone I can really see how the structure of DOE does not confound individual factors."

Hank just smiled again, thinking about Zack, the stylish analytic.

Wayne, who was also putting, said, "Hank, I really see now from the example you pointed out over the phone how DOE techniques can be beneficial in the development process. Those real examples were very insightful. I can see how examples from the books used during Six Sigma training can help communicate specific application techniques to suppliers and customers who have not yet taken the training."

Zack added, "I am thinking about how so many companies have product recall problems. It's happening in the automobile industry and computer industry quite regularly. Why aren't they using Six Sigma?"

"Interesting you said that, Zack," said Jorge as he arrived on the scene. "I've wondered the same thing. Many of these companies would say that they are implementing Six Sigma if you ask them. There must be hundreds of Six Sigma providers now popping up all over. I have to wonder how many of them are just jumping on the bandwagon. I wonder how many are implementing Six Sigma wisely."

Jorge then said, "Let me tell you what happened last month with the two projects that I have been describing. With both projects, we have identified some key process inputs that are driving our key process output. We changed our processes so that the drivers would give the most consistent response possible. In some cases we were able to error proof the process. In other cases, we created 50-Foot-Level control charts. A frequent sampling plan with these charts allowed us to identify when a special cause occurred so we could fix the problem before there was too much water under the bridge, so to speak."

"In both projects, the 30,000-Foot-Level metrics went out-of-control to the better. The process capability now looks good. We are going to track this overall process output continually. At some later date, there might be another KPIV interjected so that our overall output is degraded. With this chart we want to be able to quickly identify when this happens so that we can take appropriate action," Jorge said.

"You know, I have not really mentioned this before," Hank said, "but I found that the soft-skill training we received during the training to be very useful. This training involved people skills such as team building and change management. We also covered some creativity and project management skills."

Zack then asked, "Do you have any lessons you'd like to share from your first wave of training, Jorge?"

Jorge said, "Yes, I do. For one thing, we think that we could do a better job determining who would be the best Six Sigma Black Belt candidates. Also, we need to work at better scoping the size of our projects, and some of our metrics on some projects were not as good as they could have been. Some people were trying to force metrics into a sigma quality level format. This can lead to the wrong activity. In addition, we need to work on achieving a standard report-out format. And we want to have our suppliers more involved with our next wave of Black Belt training."

Zack then responded, "Where are you going to go from here, Jorge?"

Jorge responded, "Well, we are refining our internal process for implementing Six Sigma. When the Black Belts complete their current projects, they will be moving on to other projects. Currently, it looks like the 20 Black Belts who were in the workshop will create a total annual benefit of about ten million dollars."

Zack, then said, "Guess that got your CEO's attention."

Jorge said, "It sure did. She is planning to carry these numbers forward to the board of directors and put something in our annual report about the projects and benefits we have achieved for our customers and our shareholders."

Zack then said, "You know how I was wanting to get some face time with our CEO? Well, I could not get on his calendar. Seems like he was too busy."

Wayne said, "I was able to get in touch with our CEO at Wonder-Chem, but I don't believe that he shared my enthusiasm. He told me to get with the education department to discuss it."

Jorge then said, "I want to re-emphasize that I am sure glad that we have our CEO on board. She is very receptive and listens to our suggestions. She is getting to the point that she is asking us the right questions. As for your point, Wayne, I am really concerned about Six Sigma rollouts through the education department. This does not mean that this strategy will not work, but the image of Six Sigma when it originates from the education department is that just a bunch of tools will be taught. From this arena, it will be difficult to get visibility that Six Sigma is most successful when it is part of the strategy of a business and rolled out through those areas which are actually doing the operational tasks within a company."

Jorge continued, "And Zack, how about refocusing the intent of your meeting with your CEO? Build a case for Six Sigma by going back and collecting some of your major business metrics. I can help you put the data into a *30,000-*

Foot-Level control chart. We can then make a rough pass at the cost of doing nothing different, or CODND metrics. I'll bet that your CEO will have a 180 degree change in perspective after seeing our findings."

Hank then responded, "I agree completely with Jorge. I have a lesson learned about selling Six Sigma, too. Talk the language your CEO likes to hear: **MONEY**."

***

The round of golf that followed was another good one, or as Jorge would have described it, a second set of scores out-of-control on the good side using a *30,000-Foot-Level* control chart strategy.

For the first time in a long time, there was almost no discussion of business during the round or the dinner that followed.

It was good to relax.

Chapter 12: The 19th Hole

Take Dead Aim

This is a wonderful thought to keep in mind all the way around the course, not just on the first tee.

Take dead aim at a spot on the fairway or green, refuse to allow any negative thought to enter your head, and swing away.

Harvey Penick's Little Red Book

December

Zack was running to catch up with the others at the first tee. He called ahead excitedly, "When I took the metrics into our CEO and showed him how the COPQ was running at least 20% of our gross income, he suddenly got interested. Now I have a new job. I will be leading the corporation's new Six Sigma Business Strategy. Our rollout starts next month. This is going to be fun!"

Jorge responded. "I'm looking forward to hearing your story in the upcoming months. I must warn you though; my consulting fees will be going up considerably if you get promoted."

"That's OK," Zack smiled. "Now I have some control over my game's KPIVs. You know, my grip, stance, and

135

swing basics, ... we'll win enough golf bets to pay for them."

Zack's first tee shot backed up his boast: a nice draw about 240 yards, in the left center of the fairway. Stepping up to the tee, Wayne said, "I had a similar experience when I set up another meeting with our CEO and started speaking his language. When I put the advantages in terms of money, he bought in immediately. We are setting up the infrastructure to start our Six Sigma rollout next month as well."

Hank smiled, "Ah yes, the universal language of business executives."

Wayne continued, "I agree with Zack. After my eye surgery, I'm seeing so much better ... reading the greens and judging distances. We'll be winning more bets and collecting more of that 'universal language' from you two."

Wayne followed up his comments with boring precision. Another ho-hum performance off the tee, 265 yards straight down the middle in the perfect location.

Jorge commented, "Looks like we better step it up, partner," as Hank teed his ball. With plenty of room to work within the fairway, Hank took his driver and hit a monster drive that airmailed Wayne and Zack, leaving him in perfect birdie position.

Hank responded, "You may want to check your credit limits to see if they can handle a dinner tab, after all."

Jorge then hit his soft fade down the middle a few yards behind Zack's ball. He was the short hitter off the tee, but from this position in the fairway, with his short game, he knew that he was actually ahead of the game. He hit first from the fairway, putting his 5 wood on the green, and the pressure back firmly on the others in the group.

Jorge commented, "You know, I just realized that we are all enjoying our game much more. We all seem to be under a lot less stress."

***

In fact, Hank had resolved his Mexican production problems and had moved on to big, new cost-savings from his Six Sigma program, making Hi-tech very competitive on price while still trading on their high quality reputation. Hank had just been named Senior Vice President with new corporate-wide business improvement responsibilities. It meant fewer day-to-day headaches and more time for golf and maybe even a family life again.

Wayne had leveraged Six Sigma at Wonder-Chem, building on the previous TQM training, to create a strong competitive advantage in over-the-counter health care products. Now he was excited about Design for Six Sigma and its potential to improve R&D and reduce product development times. It had turned out that not only was Money the universal language of CEO's, but time was also money.

Zack was also making personal progress as corporate Six Sigma Champion for Z-Credit. He was finding a fertile market for business improvement in the financial sector and was beginning to build a reputation as a fast tracker again. He was even getting home most evenings before the wife and kids went to bed!

As for Jorge, he was proud that he had been able to improve Harris Hospital's performance in such a short period of time. He had kept his promise to provide his patients with the best care possible at the lowest possible cost. Now he spent most of his time coaching teams that apply the Six Sigma strategy, instead of fighting managerial fires. "Isn't it great to love your job!" he thought.

***

When the group met at Jorge's SUV in the parking lot at end of the round, everyone looked at Jorge, and Hank asked, "So when is our next golf date?"

Then Wayne and Zack chimed in, "Yes, and what's our next lesson, Professor Jorge?"

Glossary

Address: The final position, stance, and actions just before the golf swing begins.

Alignment: The position of the golfer's body and clubface in relation to the target line.

Analysis of Variance (ANOVA): A procedure to test statistically the equality of means of discrete factor inputs.

Attribute Data: The presence or absence of some characteristic.

Attribute Response: Information appraised in terms of whether a characteristic or property does or does not exist. It may be expressed as a non-compliance rate or proportion.

Away: The ball or golfer farthest from the hole is *away* and normally next to shoot.

Balanced Scorecard: A suggested scorecard that measures the business by means of the following categories:[9]
>   Financial: Return on investment and economic value-added
>   Customer: Satisfaction, retention, market, and account share
>   Internal: Quality, response time, cost, and new product introductions
>   Learning and Growth: Employee satisfaction and information system availability.

Benchmark: A standard in judging quality, value, or other important characteristics.

Best Ball: Team competition format in which the best score of any team member is recorded on each hole.

Birdie: A hole completed in one shot under par.

Bite: Describes a ball hit with backspin, which stops or backs up on the green.

Blind Hole: Any hole where the golfer cannot see the desired target area for a shot.

Bogey: A hole completed in one shot over par.

Break: The turn of a putt to the right or left as it rolls. Also, the contour of the green that causes the putt to turn.

Bump-and-Run: An approach shot to the green purposely played to hit into the face of a hill to reduce speed and then run (roll) to the hole.

Bunkers: Grass bunkers are areas on the course with severe terrain that serve as natural obstacles but are not treated as hazards. Sand or pot bunkers filled with sand are treated as hazards.

Carry: The distance a shot flies in the air. Also, to clear a hazard successfully.

Casual Water: Temporary accumulation of water on the course that is not part of the course design, as from rain or sprinklers. Balls may be lifted from casual water without penalty.

Cause and Effect Diagram: Also called the fishbone or Ishikawa diagram, the C&E Diagram is a graphical brainstorming tool used to organize possible causes (KPIVs) of a symptom into categories of causes. Standard categories are considered to be materials, machine, method, personnel, measurement, and environment. These are branched as required to additional levels. It is a tool used for gathering organizational wisdom.

Cause and Effect Matrix: A tool used to help quantify team consensus on relationships thought to exist between key input and key output variables. The results lead to other activities such as FMEA, multi-vari charts, ANOVA, regression analysis, and DOE.

Chip: Short approach shot to the green that is hit low and carries just onto the putting surface and then bounces and rolls to the hole. Also, chip and run.

Comebacker: The putt back to the hole after the previous putt has run past the hole.

Common Cause: Natural or random variation that is inherent in a process over time, affecting every outcome of the process. If a process is in-control, it has common cause variation only. If a process operates at an unsatisfactory level, chronic problems result. For this situation, the process is said to be not capable (of meeting specification needs).

Confidence Interval: The limits or band of a parameter that contains the true parameter value at a confidence level. The band can be single-sided to describe an upper/lower limit or double-sided to describe both upper and lower limits.

Continuous Response: A response is said to be continuous if any value can be taken between limits. Examples include weight, distance, and voltage.

Control Chart: A procedure used to track a process over time for the purpose of determining if data are common or special cause.

C_p: A process capability index metric used to specify how well a process is performing relative to customer requirements or specification(s). It is affected by the variation in the process relative to its specification. A larger C_p number indicates the process has less process variability relative to the width of a specification.

C_{pk}: A process capability index metric used to specify how well a process is performing relative to customer requirements or specification(s). It is affected by both the variation in the process and by how well centered that variation is within the specification. A larger C_{pk} number indicates the process is performing better.

Dead (or Stiff): A shot right at the hole, especially if it stops close to the hole.

Divots: The piece of turf taken by a proper iron swing.

DOE (Design of Experiments): Experiment methodology in which factor levels are assessed in a fractional factorial experiment or in a full factorial experiment structure.

Dogleg: A hole where the fairway bends to the right or left. Also, the area where a fairway bends.

DMAIC: These are the five phases of Six Sigma.

Define – Define and scope the project.

Measure – Define smart metrics and baseline the project. Establish current, high-level metrics for the process, including the capability of the process. Consider measurement system analysis.

Analyze – Use Six Sigma analysis tools to find root causes. Evaluate relationships between input factors and output responses, and model processes.

Improve – Optimize processes.

Control – Institutionalize and maintain gains.

Double Bogie: A hole completed in two shots over par.

DPMO: (Defects per Million Opportunities) Number of defects that, on average, occur in one million opportunities. Care should be taken to assure that all defects, including touch-ups and reworks that previously may not have been recorded, are included in this calculation. Also important is an agreed-upon standard method for counting opportunities.

Drop Area: When a ball is hit into a hazard and cannot be played as it lies, it may be dropped and played from designated *drop areas*, with the appropriate penalty.

Draw: A shot that turns slightly from right to left in flight for a right-handed golfer. Also, the deliberate attempt to play a controlled shot that has *draw*. Not to be confused with a *hook*, a shot with excessive right to left movement for a right-handed golfer.

Enough Club: Slang for the proper club to carry a given yardage and not end up *short*.

Fade: A shot that turns slightly from left to right in flight for a right-handed golfer. Also, the deliberate attempt to play a controlled shot that has *fade*. Not to be confused with a *slice*, a shot with excessive left to right to left movement for a right-handed golfer.

Fat: A shot that strikes the ground before impacting the ball. Often takes too much turf (too big a divot) and ends up short of the intended target.

50-Foot-Level Metric: A low-level metric or KPIV, which can affect the response of a *30,000-Foot-Level* Metric.

5S: Procedures used to clean up and organize a work place (housekeeping): Sort, Straighten, Shine, Standardize Work, and Sustain Improvements.

FMEA (Failure Mode and Effect Analysis): A proactive method of improving reliability and minimizing failures in a product or service. It is an analytical approach to preventing problems in processes. For a process FMEA, Wisdom of the Organization is used to list what can go wrong at each step of a process that could cause potential failures or customer problems. Each item is evaluated for its importance, frequency of occurrence, and probability of detecting its occurrence. This information is used to prioritize the items that most need improving. These are then assigned a corrective action plan to reduce their risk.

Fire-Fighting: The practice of giving much focus to fixing the *problems of the day*. The usual corrective actions taken in fire-fighting, such as tweaking a stable process, do not create any long-term fixes and may actually cause degradation to the process.

Free Drop (or Relief): Slang for allowance to move the ball to an unobstructed position without penalty, e.g., from casual water or ground under repair.

Fringe: The close-cut grass surrounding the green. Also known as the apron, frog hair, or collar.

Gage R&R (Repeatability and Reproducibility): A tool used in Measurement System Analysis. It is the evaluation of measuring instruments to determine their capability to yield a precise response. It determines how much of the observed process variation is due to measurement system variation. Gage repeatability is the variation in measurements using the same measurement instrument several times by one appraiser measuring the identical characteristic on the same part. Gage reproducibility is the variation in the average of measurements made by different appraisers using the same measuring instrument when measuring the identical characteristics on the same part.

Green, Fast vs. Slow: Greens that are cut short or are dry and hard are typically *fast*. Putts will go farther than normal and break more on fast greens. Greens that grow longer, or are wet and soft, are often *slow*. Putts will go shorter than normal and break less on slow greens. Putts may also be referred to as *fast* or *slow*.

Grain: The direction that the grass grows, which may affect the speed and break of putts. Putts hit with the *grain* will roll farther and break less than putts against the *grain*.

Ground under Repair: Marked areas of the course where maintenance is being performed. Balls landing in these areas may be dropped without penalty out of the marked area but no nearer the hole.

Ground Your Club: Touching the ground with the club. Grounding the club is normally permitted, but a penalty is received for grounding the club in a hazard.

Halved: A hole is halved in scoring when teams or golfers tie on that hole.

Handicap: A system to rank golfers according to their skill levels, allowing them to engage fairly in even competition.

Hazard: Lakes, streams, ponds, creeks, ditches, bunkers, or nature areas on the golf course may be marked as *hazards*. Balls may be played from within the *hazards* or dropped out of the *hazards* with appropriate penalties.

Histogram: A graphical representation or bar graph of the sample relative frequency distribution describing the occurrence of grouped items. This graph summarizes and displays the distribution of data in an easier-to-grasp form than tables of data.

Hole Out: To complete the final stroke into the cup or hole.

Home: A shot that lands on the green is said to get *home*; e.g. get *home* in two.

Honor: The player with the lowest score on the previous hole has the *honor* on the next hole. *Honors* carry over on ties.

In Regulation: The ideal score (par) on a hole minus two putts; i.e., the ideal number of strokes allowed to reach the green in regulation. For example, on a par four hole, getting on the green in two shots would be *in regulation*.

ISO-9000:2000: An updated version of ISO-9000. It requires that you demonstrate improvements are being made within your processes.

ISO-9000: ISO-9000 consists of individual but related international standards on quality management and quality assurance. Developed to help companies effectively document the quality-system elements to be implemented in order to maintain an efficient quality system. It is a requirement often placed on manufacturing companies. The basic idea behind ISO-9000 methodology is that you document what you do and you do what you say. During an ISO-9000 certification process, the examining registrar will audit your company to confirm that you are following the standard. If you are, you can be certified.

Kaizen Event (or Kaizen Blitz): Kaizen is a Japanese term meaning gradual unending improvement by doing little things better and setting and achieving increasingly higher standards. A *Kaizen Event* occurs when an operation team works together to improve a specific operation. It typically involves a detailed description of the current state of the selected operation, developing the Kaizen plan for improvement, implementing the plan, following-up to confirm that the plan was carried out fully and correctly, and reporting to management on the event and its accomplishments.

Kanban: Pulling a product through the production process. This method of manufacturing process-flow-control only allows movement of material by pulling from a preceding process. Inventory is kept low. When quality errors are detected, there is less product affected.

KPIV (Key Process Input Variable): Factors within a process correlated to an output characteristic(s) important to the internal or external customer. Optimizing and controlling these is vital to the improvement of the KPOV.

KPOV (Key Process Output Variable): Characteristic(s) of the output of a process that are important to the customer. Understanding what is important to the internal and external customer is essential to identifying KPOVs.

Lag: A conservative attempt to get close enough to (often short of) the hole so that the next putt can be made. The opposite of a bold putt that may go far past the hole and leave a difficult second putt.

Lateral Water Hazard: A water hazard that runs parallel to the length of a hole, typically defined by red lines or stakes. Drops from this require a one-stroke penalty.

Lay Up: A strategic shot played short of the green or hazard intended to leave a safe play on the next shot.

Lean: An approach to producing products or services focusing on reducing total cycle time and costs by reducing waste, improving flow, and striving for excellence.

Lean Enterprise: Focusing on the identification and reduction of waste throughout the entire organization and involving both suppliers and customers in the effort.

Lean Manufacturing: A manufacturing process involving tools such as value-stream mapping and workflow diagrams without considering either supplier or customer processes. The methodology used to implement the Lean production philosophy.

Left Edge, Right Edge: The left or right edges of the hole or green may be used as aiming targets when allowing for the break or the wind.

Lie: The position of the ball in the grass (good, buried, tight, fluffy) or relative to the terrain (level, uphill, downhill, side hill). Also, the angle of the club head to the shaft (upright, standard, or flat).

Long Irons: Typically 1, 2, 3, and 4 irons.

Malcolm Baldrige Award: An award established by U.S. Congress in 1987 to raise awareness of quality management and to recognize companies that have implemented successful quality management systems. Its name comes from the late Secretary of Commerce, Malcolm Baldrige, a proponent of quality management.

Malcolm Baldrige Assessment: The process of assessing how well an organization performs to the Baldrige criteria. Organizations often use the criteria to self-assess their performance. There are seven categories:

> Leadership
> Strategic Planning
> Customer and Market Focus
> Information and Analysis
> Human Resource Development
> Process Management
> Business Results.

Makable: A shot with a realistic chance of being made successfully.

Matches: Games, league competitions, or wagers.

Match Play: Competition format in which the winner is determined by the number of holes won rather than by total strokes (stroke play).

MBA: Master of Business Administration.

Mean: Sum of all responses divided by the sample size.

Measurement Systems Analysis: Analysis of the complete process of obtaining measurements. This includes the collection of equipment, operations, procedures, software, and personnel that affects the assignment of a number to a measurement characteristic. Includes, but is not limited to, Gage R&R.

Muda: A Japanese term indicating efforts that do not add value (waste). Some categories of *muda* are defects, over production or excess inventory, idle time, and poor layout

Mulligan: A second chance or gratuitous replay of a shot, normally reserved for informal outings.

Multi-vari chart: A chart that displays the variance within units, between units, between samples, and between lots. It is useful in detecting variation sources within a process.

Nearest Point of Relief: The nearest point that is no closer to the hole, where relief may be taken whenever a drop is permitted.

Net: Score on a hole or round after the handicap has been deducted from the gross score.

Obstructions: Man-made objects such as cart paths, benches, etc. that are not part of the course design. Typically, a free drop may be given when a golfer's ball, stance, or shot path is impeded by an obstruction.

Order of Play: Normally, the order of play at the tee goes to the golfer or team who won the previous hole. On the first tee, the order of play is often determined by chance. After tee shots, order of play is determined by who is farthest away from the hole. Ready golf is a popular alternative, designed to speed up the game, in which the order of play is determined by which golfers are ready to hit.

Organizational Wisdom: Wisdom about a process that comes intuitively from past experience of team members. It is used to provide possible solutions to problems, which are then evaluated by appropriate analysis tools.

Out: The ball or player farthest from the hole. Also **away**.

Out-of-Bounds (OB): A ball that has gone beyond the designated area of play for the hole (normally marked by white stakes). When a ball is hit OB in tournament competition, the golfer must play another ball from the original spot with a one-stroke penalty. In recreational play, it is customary for the new ball to be dropped just inside the fairway closest to where the ball left the fairway with a one-stroke penalty.

Pairing: Players scheduled to play together as competitors or partners.

Par: The regulation number of strokes set for a hole played perfectly, determined by yardage and hole design.

Passive Analysis: Data collected and analyzed as the process is currently performing to determine potential KPIVs. Process alterations are not assessed.

PGA Tour: The series of Professional Golfers Association Tournaments.

Pick Up: Picking up a ball before the hole is completed. In match play or recreational play, a golfer may tell an opponent to "pick it up". Not applicable in stroke play competition.

Pin Placement: Hole location on the green. A pin placed in the middle of a large green may be called an *easy* pin placement, while one hidden close behind a bunker is called a *tough* or *sucker* pin placement.

Pitch: A short, high approach shot into the green, which lands softly and doesn't roll too far.

Pitch In or Chip In: A pitch or chip shot that goes directly into the hole from off the green.

PPM (Parts per Million): An attribute measurement of defect rate, expressed in defects found divided by one million. Percent defects were once the standard. Note that a percentage-unit-improvement in parts-per-million (ppm) defect rate does not equate to the same percentage improvement in the sigma quality level.

PPMO (Parts per Million Opportunities): A defect-per-unit calculation giving additional insight into a process by including the number of opportunities for failure. When this is done, the metric is DPMO. Care must be taken in estimating the number of opportunities for defects in a process.

Probability Plot: Data are plotted on a selected probability coordinate system to determine if a particular distribution is appropriate and to make statements about percentiles of the population.

Poka-Yoke: A Japanese term indicating a mechanism that either prevents a mistake from occurring or makes a mistake obvious at a glance.

Process Capability: A measure of the ability of a process to produce output that is within the customer requirement or specification. Two frequently encountered metrics of process capability are C_p and C_{pk}.

Putt Out: To putt the ball into the hole. Also, to continue putting after the first putt, even if the golfer is not *away*.

Putting Line: The line a putt follows to the hole on the green, determined by the slope and contour of the green.

Reading a Putt: The act of estimating the speed and line of a putt before putting.

Regression or Regression Analysis: A defined process for quantifying and modeling the response (KPOV) of a process relative to its input variables. It estimates the relationship between KPIVs and the KPOV of a process and produces a mathematical model of that relationship. Its use can lead to a better understanding of the critical factors controlling the quality of the process output.

Relief: Shots that come to rest in an obstruction or *ground under repair* may be entitled to *relief*. See **Free Drop**.

Robust Process: A process is considered robust when its output variability is not sensitive to the normal variation from its input variables. For example, a manufacturing process step is robust to different operators who normally execute the operation step.

Rough: The area of the course off the fairway, not in a hazard, where the grass is often allowed to grow taller.

Sand Traps: Hazards filled with sand. They are often positioned close to landing areas either near the fairway or the green.

Satellite-Level Metric: A high-level metric of a business process. It can separate common cause from special cause variation. It can reduce fire-fighting activities and improve the focus of improvement efforts.

Scoring: The grooves on the face of the club, especially irons. It may also refer to the act of shooting low scores.

Scramble: A team competition in which all team members hit their shot and choose the best ball position from which to shoot their next round of shots. This is repeated until the team holes out.

Scratch: A term used to describe a golfer who shoots par or has a zero handicap.

Short Game: Approach shots and putts. The part of the game that is typically inside approximately 100 yards from the hole.

Short Hitter: A player who doesn't hit the ball far or hits shortest off the tee.

Short Irons: Typically the 7, 8, and 9 irons, and the pitching, gap, sand, and lob wedges.

Sigma Quality Level: A metric calculated by some to describe the capability of a process relative to its specification. A six sigma quality level is said to have a 3.4 ppm rate.

Skin: A game in which an amount is bet on each hole, e.g., dime skins. The lowest score on a hole wins, but if two players tie, all tie, and the pot rolls over until someone records a skin.

S.M.A.R.T.: An acronym for guidelines used in creating goals and strategies.

      S – Specific

      M – Measurable

      A – Agreed upon and Attainable

      R – Realistic and Rewarded

      T – Timely.

Special Cause: Variation in a process from a cause that is not an inherent part of that process. That is, it's not a common cause.

Standard Deviation: A mathematical quantity that quantifies the variability of a response.

Starter: Course employee in charge of tee times.

Thin: A shot that catches the ball with the sole of the club. *Thin* shots may damage the ball or produce uncontrolled low shots.

Tee Box: The tee area at the start of each hole.

Tees, Red, White, or Blue: Within a tee box, red tees indicate positions from which ladies tee off. White tees are commonly used by average players. Blue tees may be championship tees. Other colors may be used, depending on local course convention. Tee colors indicate the starting position for players who have different skill levels.

Theory of Constraints (TOC): Eliyahu Goldratt describes in his book, *The Goal*,[7] a model that challenges many traditional accounting and business practices. He makes the case that we often do not know what our true business goal is. One goal every business shares is the need to be profitable. A particular business will have other goals as well. These goals must be well thought out, clearly stated, and communicated to everyone in the organization. Goldratt's procedures focus on three metrics: throughput (the rate at which the system produces income), inventory (all the money the system invests in things to sell as well as all money tied up in the system), and operating expense (money spent turning inventory into throughput). The constraints that prevent achieving our goal(s) are primarily system restraints. Therefore, we must determine what to change, what to change to, and how to cause change. Goldratt describes five sequential steps to remove constraints and progress toward a goal:

1. Identify the system Constraint
2. Decide how to exploit the Constraint
3. Subordinate everything else
4. Elevate the Constraint
5. Go back to step one

30,000-Foot-Level Metric: – A high-level, big-picture, long-term measure of an operational or project process metric used in a Six Sigma strategy. A *30,000-Foot-Level* control chart would be used to separate common cause variation in a process from special cause. This metric can improve the understanding of process variation and can redirect fire-fighting activities (i.e., reacting to all unsatisfactory output as if it were a special cause) to fire-prevention activities (i.e., using a team to systematically improve the process through a Six Sigma strategy). This measurement can be used to baseline a process before beginning a Six Sigma project and then to track the project's progress.

Total Quality Management (TQM): There are many definitions of this term. It is an approach to quality that uses management practices and quality tools to improve quality continuously to customers. It is believed that the term was initially coined in 1985 by the Naval Air Systems Command to describe its Japanese-style management approach to quality improvement. The methods used are gleaned from the teachings of quality leaders such as Deming, Juran, Feigenbaum, Crosby, and Ishikawa. Feigenbaum originated the concept of total quality control in his book *Total Quality Control*, published in 1951.

Touch and Feel: The ability in putting and the short-game to judge conditions and distances in order to get close to the hole.

Triple Bogey: A hole completed in three shots over par.

Trouble: Balls that do not land on the fairway or green as intended are said to be in *trouble*.

Turn: The start of the back nine is often called the *turn*. Historically, older links courses used to go out in one direction for nine holes and make the turn before coming back to the clubhouse.

Two-Putt: The standard allowance for putting when computing par. Taking two putts to complete the hole once the ball reaches the green.

Unplayable Lie: A ball in a position that cannot be played, as determined by the player. Standard rules for *relief* with penalty apply.

Water Hazard: Any marked body of water that is played as a hazard, usually defined by yellow lines or stakes. The ball may be played from the hazard or dropped behind the hazard with a two-stroke penalty.

References

1. *Implementing Six Sigma: Smarter Solutions using Statistical Methods*, Forrest W. Breyfogle III, Wiley, New York, 1999.
2. *Managing Six Sigma: A Practical Guide to Understanding, Assessing, and Implementing the Strategy That Yields Bottom-Line Success*, Forrest W. Breyfogle III, James M. Cupello, Becki Meadows, Wiley, New York, 2001.
3. www.smartersolutions.com
4. "Bottom-line Success with Six Sigma," Forrest W. Breyfogle III and Becki Meadows, *Quality Progress*, pp. 101-104, May 2001.
5. *Fifth Discipline: The Art and Practice of the Learning Organization*, Peter Senge, Doubleday/Current, New York, 1990.
6. *Statistical Methods for Testing, Development, and Manufacturing*, Forrest W. Breyfogle III, Wiley, New York, 1992.
7. *The Goal*, 2nd ed., E. M. Goldratt, North River Press, New York, 1992.
8. *Harvey Penick's Little Red Book*, Harvey Penick with Bud Shrake, Simon and Schuster, 1992.
9. *The Balanced Scorecard*, Robert S. Kaplan and David P. Norton, Harvard Business School Press, Boston, 1996.

About the Authors

Forrest W. Breyfogle III

Forrest W. Breyfogle III is a Professional Engineer, ASQ (American Society for Quality) Certified Quality Engineer and Reliability Engineer, and an ASQ Fellow. He has conducted many Six Sigma training and coaching sessions throughout the world. He has taught classes or conducted external workshops for many professional societies, including Society of Manufacturing Engineers (SME), American Society for Quality (ASQ), and Association for Manufacturing Excellence (AME).

David Enck

David has eight years of experience as a Master Black Belt and over 15 years of experience with measurement capability, statistical process control, and design of experiments for process and product development in a variety of industries. He has worked with flexible circuits, medical devices, IC manufacturing and environmental assessment. In addition to his extensive industrial experience, David has broad teaching experience that includes three years of lecturing in the Statistics Department at the University of Florida and teaching DFSS and process characterization methods to all levels of a business operation, from VP to operator.

David is a Ph.D. candidate (A.B.D.) in Industrial and Systems Engineering, with a minor in Statistics, from the University of Florida at Gainesville. He holds both an M.A. and a B.A. in Statistics, with an emphasis in Computer Science and Engineering, from SUNY at Buffalo, New York.

Phil Flories

Phil is an instructor and course developer for Smarter Solutions. Previously, he spent 25 years with Motorola as a Quality Engineer. Phil is a certified lead examiner for QS9000 (Lloyds). His ASQ certifications include Certified Quality Engineer, Certified Quality Manager, and Certified Quality Auditor. He also prepares and teaches ASQ certification preparation classes (CQE, CQT, CMI, CQA, CQM).

Phil has served with the Texas Quality Award, six years on the panel of judges and seven years training examiners. He lives in the Austin, Texas area with his wife and three children.

Thomas A. Pearson

Tom Pearson is a Technical Fellow and co-founder of Praedictus Corporation, an Indianapolis company that provides predictive process management software tools and methods for real-time operations management and business improvement. Tom received his BA in Physics and

Mathematics from University of Indianapolis and MS in Operations Research from The George Washington University. Tom is a systems scientist, designer, consultant, speaker, and author in the field of business improvement and information systems. He co-holds US patents for Real-Time Quality Management and Entity Relation Data Base software. He also designed the Exploratory Quality Control software and co-authored the Exploratory Quality Control Handbook. Tom was elected a Fellow in the American Society for Quality in 1998, and completed his S^4 Black Belt training in 1999.

Acknowledgements

The authors thank Becki Meadows and Dorothy Stewart for their excellent editorial inputs, Jewell Parker for book title idea, and Kathy Flories for her input on character development. We thank Gerry Balden and Leanne Dillingham for their up-front publishing guidance. We also thank Kim Harrington for her diligence in expediting our publishing process.

For their voice-of-the-customer input during the development process of our book, the authors thank Bob Ashenbrenner, Maury Ayrer, Bill Baker, Bob Bolton, Fred Bothwell, Becki Breyfogle, Dan Breyfogle, Wes Breyfogle, Holland Brown, Jerry Coad, Betsi Ehrlich, Mike Gettinger, Chuck James, David Ladensohn, David Laney, John McCool, Todd Minnick, Keith Moe, Dave Quaglieri, David Schwartz, Rick Simon, and Gary Url.

For the cover design, we thank Jorge Calderon and Laverne Johnson of the International Institute of Learning, Inc.

Our Other Books

Implementing Six Sigma: Smarter Solutions using Statistical Methods, Forrest W. Breyfogle III, Wiley, 1999.

Managing Six Sigma: A Practical Guide to Understanding, Assessing, and Implementing the Strategy That Yields Bottom Line Success, Forrest W. Breyfogle III, James M. Cupello, Becki Meadows, Wiley, 2001.

Statistical Methods for Testing, Development, and Manufacturing, Forrest W. Breyfogle III, Wiley, 1992.

What Others Have Said

"What makes [*Implementing Six Sigma*] significant is you do not have to be an expert in statistics or even in the Quality field to understand and implement the tools of Six Sigma. ...." - Susan May, North Little Rock, Arkansas, USA

"...We at GE have made Six Sigma part of our culture and a way of doing business. If you are already a six sigma company or thinking about becoming one, ... I recommend that you get a copy of this book [*Implementing Six Sigma*]. It is a winner! winner!" - David Wilson, USA

"…[*Implementing Six Sigma*] is the best single volume on statistics-oriented Six Sigma methodologies that I have come across so far." - T. N. Goh, Singapore

"…Project management is made simple with Forrest's 21 steps for project integration of tools found on page 18. This book [*Implementing Six Sigma*] is geared towards practitioners of Six-Sigma. If you are a plant manager, buy this book for your quality and engineering managers. This book was written with integrity. Thanks, Forrest." - John Knickel, Ohio, USA

"…. the most complete and well-written resource on the subject that I have seen. The subject arrangement and language is clear and concise. Thanks, Mr. Breyfogle. "
- Norman Whitmire

"I am asked all of the time if there is a book that Executives and Business Leaders can read to understand what Six Sigma is all about and to help determine if it is right for their organizations. Until now, I had to give them a list of books that would come close if they read them all. This is THE one. This book [*Managing Six Sigma*] clearly establishes its objectives and nails them." - Bill Dean, Allen, TX

About Smarter Solutions, Inc

www.smartersolutions.com
13776 U.S. Highway 183 N., Suite 122-110
Austin, TX 78750-1811
512-918-0280

Forrest W. Breyfogle III founded Smarter Solutions in 1992 after a 24-year career at IBM. Mr. Breyfogle began his career with IBM as an engineer in development and later transferred to a product test organization. Within these organizations, he became very interested in the benefits resulting from the wise use of statistical techniques. In 1980, Mr. Breyfogle requested that a full-time position be created for him within IBM as an internal statistical consultant. From 1980 to 1992 Mr. Breyfogle served IBM in this capacity, applying Six Sigma methodology to testing, development, manufacturing, and service organizations.

Mr. Breyfogle has authored or co-authored *Statistical Methods for Testing, Development, and Manufacturing*, Wiley, 1992, *Implementing Six Sigma*, Wiley, 1999, and *Managing Six Sigma*, Wiley, 2001.

Mr. Breyfogle's first book, *Statistical Methods for Testing, Development, and Manufacturing*[6], was written to illustrate the benefits and how-tos of *wisely* applied statistical methodologies. This book, published in 1992, includes a 10-step Six Sigma implementation roadmap.

Mr. Breyfogle and the Smarter Solutions, Inc. team have conducted many Six Sigma workshop sessions throughout the world. On-site and public training/coaching sessions include Green Belt, Black Belt, Design for Six Sigma (DFSS), Lean Six Sigma, Champion, and Executive training sessions. They have coached many individuals and organizations on the wise application of Six Sigma techniques. In 2001 Mr. Breyfogle was selected as the Six Sigma Subject Matter Expert (SME) for a Six Sigma Benchmarking study orchestrated by APQC.

Members of the Smarter Solutions team are proud of the feedback that they have received on their training and training material, which is made robust to differences that occur in the experience of both workshop attendees and instructors.

Notes

Notes